Single Woman
CHRONICLES

AN ATLANTA LOVE STORY...KINDA

· ASHLEIGH GUICE ·

ISBN-13: 978-1985206021
ISBN-10: 1985206021

Cover and interior typesetting by Vanessa Mendozzi

First Edition First Printing

Contents

CHAPTER 1

You're Single...Act as Such

Another Valentine's Day alone. This is really starting to get old. How is someone that's caramel, 5' 9", thicker than a Snicker with abs like Yoncé in the 90s, and dress game sicker than Traci Ellis Ross from Girlfriends still single? On top of that, I have my own tax business making over $75,000 a year. There is no way my ass should be single. I am the full package. I'm starting to think I'm cursed.

Since I was young, I have always been the single friend. Girls were constantly jealous of me growing up because they swore I wanted their man, but really their man wanted me. Crazy because all I wanted was a man of my own. I went to prom with a guy I said yes to at the last minute because my crush was going with someone else. I never had a high school sweetheart or a college boo thang. And here I am, 28, doomed to be single forever.

WHY ME LORD?!!

My cell phone went off on my nightstand and I leaned over to get it, trying not to fall out of my California king bed.

> Marbles: Happy Valentine's Day! Let me take you out to lunch or something.

Ugh! Another text from Marbles. When will he realize I don't want him? I tried to let him down easily by just ignoring all or most of his text messages and saying no to all his dinner invitations, but he just keeps on messaging me. I don't have the heart to tell him he doesn't have a chance. Maybe lunch with him won't be so bad, I mean I am super lonely on Valentine's Day.

> Arianna: Hey! Happy V Day. That sounds good, around what time are you thinking?

I know it's wrong to go out with someone you're really not interested in, but we both benefit. He gets to see me, and I get gifts and free lunch. This is a win/win situation. Being single as long as I have, you learn to just accept what you can get. I get approached by many men and I have gone on several dates, but the people I really want never work out. It's like as soon as I start dating them and we get to that blissful honeymoon stage, where we're talking all day and seeing each other every weekend, something goes wrong. Every single time I let my guard down, they start getting distant, then poof they're gone. I vow to not let my guard down anymore! At least until they've proven themselves worthy.

    Marbles: Great, I'll pick you up around
    3PM. Wear something sexy.

Did that fool just tell me to wear something sexy? You see this is how he got his nickname.

In the single world, there are a few unwritten rules.

Rule #1: Everyone has a nickname until they become official. It gets hard for your friends to keep up sometimes, so you nickname them by their actions. Marbles got his nickname because he is missing a few. He is actually very attractive and could have been great boyfriend material, but he is as deep as a puddle.

Rule #2: Never save phone numbers under pet names unless you're in an actual relationship. When you save it under a pet name like "Booskie" or "Bae", it's like men get this alert that they have you right where they want you and then they start acting up. Don't let them win, save them under their government name just in case you forget their name. Don't save them under their nickname because you never want them to see it and have to explain it.

Rule #3: Never assume you're in a relationship. Until the guy makes it official, you are single until professed otherwise. If he has not verbally said "Will you be my girlfriend?" then you are single and you should act as such.

Rule #4: To every guy you date, he is the only one. Women are not like men and we can't date five dudes at once and be respected. To him, he is your knight in shining armor and you are taking your time to get to know him. If he asks about other guys, you just deflect and tell him he's all you're thinking about because at that moment, you're telling the truth. If he makes it to boyfriend, then you proceed to cut everyone off and he will actually be the only one. Until then, you are single and should act as such.

Rule #5: Date who you want and have fun with it. Just because you're a woman doesn't mean you have to date one guy at a time. Juggle as many as you can handle, but to them, they are the only one. You are single and should act as such.

Rule #6: You screw one person at a time. Aids and babies are real, so act like you know. Give the cookie to the most deserving gentleman and be a nun to the others. You could just have a "friend with benefits" on the side while you figure it out, but safety first. Birth control and condoms preferably because no one has time for aids and babies.

Rule #7: Act like a lady, and think like a man. Steve Harvey was not lying in that book. If you have been single for a while, you have probably bumped your head numerous times. To avoid that, you must think like them but still maintain your elegance. Move like a gazelle, but attack like a tiger.

Rule #8: YOU ARE SINGLE SO AND SHOULD ACT AS SUCH. Pretty self-explanatory but must be repeated because most women tend to move too quickly with men and need to learn that they are still single and need to act that way. If he has not purchased the cow, don't give him the milk. Be your best single self.

There are far more unwritten rules, but those are my main ones. It's tough out here being single, but someone has to do it. And since I have to live it, I may as well live it up. I have been through way too much with men to not follow the rules I have set for myself. They better get with this program, or get lost. I will move to this beat until someone comes to take me off the market. I hope God is listening because I need that to happen like ASAP. I am so tired of going out with losers like Marbles because I am bored and lonely. I need my Russel Wilson or Devon Franklin to come on.

A hard knock at the door interrupted my thoughts.

"Who is it?!" I yelled, as I made my way to the door to see who was knocking like the police.

Once I reached the door, I looked through the peephole to see my best friend standing at the door with something behind her back. I snatched the door open.

"Bianca, what the hell is wrong with you knocking like the po pos?!"

"I would've just come in, but I left my key at home. But don't be rude to me, I know your momma raised you better." Bianca said, as she brushed passed me heading to the couch.

Bianca was one of my best friends. We met while working together in a restaurant a few years ago and had been inseparable ever since. We even lived in the same apartment complex. I don't even know how we ended up being friends; she was the complete opposite of me. She didn't drink, she didn't go out to clubs, and when she dated, she actually dated one man at a time. Me on the other hand, drank like sailor, dated at least three men at a time, and will twerk with the best of them at MJQ on a Friday night. I guess it's true what they say, opposites do attract because I love that girl. She brought out my sensible side and I really appreciated her for it.

"What are you hiding behind your back?" I probed, grabbing Bianca's arm trying to figure out what she had up her sleeve.

"Ugh, you so nosey," she rolled her eyes, slowly revealing the surprise. She brought her arm from behind her back displaying my favorite red velvet cupcake from Camicakes Cupcakes.

"No you didn't get me a Camicakes!" I shouted, running to get my delectable treat.

"Happy V Day" she smiled as she handed me my cupcake.

"You're the sweetest person ever! I promise I'd marry you if DeWayne didn't beat me to the punch. No homo though." I walked to the kitchen to grab a fork to dig into my cupcake.

"Girl, I still can't believe I'm engaged! I never saw that coming. Last year, you and I both were single and spent V Day over ice cream and Golden Girls; a year later I am engaged to be married. Crazy how God works! Ain't he good girl?" Bianca emphasized as she raised her hands in the air giving glory to God.

I was so happy for her. Contrary to popular belief, you can be one hundred percent happy for someone even when you aren't happy with your own situation. If anyone deserved to be engaged to a good man like Dewayne, it's Bianca. She was beautiful. She stood 5'4" with the richest chocolate skin and a body that would make a blind man wink. What made this even better was that she was one of the nicest and most genuine people I had ever met. To top it off, she had been celibate for five years before her engagement. I applauded her so much for that because in a society that praises sex before marriage, saving yourself can be tough. She withheld from sex and didn't budge even after men criticized her for the decision to do it God's way. It was a great choice to make because when she met DeWayne, she realized it was all worth it. She had been blessed with an incredible fiancé and I couldn't wait to plan her bachelorette party. I know she was nervous because I told her we weren't going to do anything I wouldn't do, which leaves everything.

"Ain't he though! He needs to stop playing and lift this curse off my life. I know he doomed me to be single forever bruh." I was instantly reminded of my current reality. I dropped my head and took a bite from my cupcake beginning to get sad again.

"Girl you're not cursed; you just need the right guy. You know the men you pick aren't the best and you juggle too many to even know if someone could be the one," she counseled, making eye contact with me to display her sincerity. "I keep telling you that you need to stop playing and be celibate, and pray for your husband like I did."

"I should be ce- what? How Sway? Sex ain't did nothing to me but bring me pleasure. You want me to give that up and wait one hundred years for my curse to be lifted? Oh hells no."

"You're gonna listen to me one day."

"Welp, today ain't that day. I need to go get ready for this free lunch with Marbles anyway," I announced, immediately regretting what I had just said. She did not like Marbles one bit.

Bianca swiftly turned her head towards me in shock, "You're going out with Marbles?! Girl, why do you keep wasting your time with people who don't even deserve to be in your presence?!"

"B, you don't understand. I have been alone on V Day for like six years now. He asked, so why not? I'm tired of being lonely. Marbles would never be my first pick, but at least he thought about me enough to even want to make me his valentine. More than I can say for those losers in the past."

I got up from my kitchen barstool and went into my room to find something to wear. Bianca followed me. "But Arianna, who cares that it's V Day. Before my DeWayne, I spent it alone for just as long as you. You weren't alone last year, I was there. This day is just like any other day. What's wrong with spending it alone and just relaxing, something you rarely ever do?"

"Everything is wrong with it! I am almost thirty with no prospect of a husband in sight. I am cursed and my batteries on my vibrator are low. I gotta get out in the world and find me a man. You're engaged, you don't know this life anymore." I grumbled as I went through my closet sifting through clothes.

"But Arianna, be real with yourself. Stop saying you're cursed, you're the reason you're single. You date multiple men and no one is good enough. Then, when you find one that is good enough, you move too quickly, ultimately pushing him away. You're beautiful, talented, and you're a boss. You have to start acting like it in order to attract a man who is worthy of that. You gotta stop giving your time to men like Marbles, who thinks escargot is a luggage company."

I take a deep breath to muster up the energy to respond to another best friend lecture. "Brrrruuuuhhhhh, I don't need this today. First of all, what the hell is escargot? Second of all, it's just a free meal and possibly gifts. I don't care about Marbles. I wouldn't count this as giving him time because I couldn't care less about him. I'm just bored and he's there. Let me be cheered up by free food and gifts."

There's an awkward silence in the room. Bianca drops her head then shakes it. "You just don't get it. God will never send you a man when you already have five. I don't care if they are just there for kicks and giggles, or for entertainment, that's just not how God works. Until you position yourself for Mr. Right, you will constantly attract Mr. Wrong."

I stop rummaging through my clothes and come out of my closet to face Bianca. I see the seriousness in her eyes, as she looks at me as if she wants to cry. She has been my friend for over five years now and I know she loves me. She has seen me hurt time and time again by men and has always been by my side to help me pick up the pieces. I know she only wants what's best for me, but I just feel like she doesn't understand me sometimes. Bianca is naturally a home body who doesn't like to go out and doesn't like getting to know new people, whereas I am naturally the life of the party that just goes with the flow. I know I'm not always right, but I don't believe I have to use her formula to find my Mr. Right. She should just let me live my life how I want to live it and not judge me. I don't judge her.

"B, I know you love me and want what's best, but you gotta let me live my life. I hear everything you're saying, but I'm not you. I can't be celibate or just wait. I'm single and I feel that I should act single. Men don't wait around for Ms. Right, they go do their thing until they find one they like. I'm just trying to have fun, and not be depressed while I wait." I explained, looking at her straight in the eyes hoping this would end my thirty ninth "Why the way I single is wrong" lecture.

"You're right, it is your life. I just know you, and I see things you don't see. But I'm your best friend so you know I have to keep it all the way real with you. Either way, I'm here regardless. But go ahead and have your little pity lunch with Marbles. Hopefully he knows how to read the menu this time." She snickered, recalling my last date disaster with Marbles.

"That was one time, and it was an Italian restaurant. The menu was hard to read. Plus, he had it upside down," I laughed, throwing a shirt at her.

"Well, let me go. I gotta go get cute and prepare for whatever my fiancé has planned. I have a fiancé; it still feels weird to say." Bianca beams as she gets up to head towards the door.

"Have fun, girl! I know you not doin' the nasty 'til

your wedding day, but you can still put that booty on 'em to show him what he gone get," I twerked a little then dropped it to the floor and brung it back up. What can I say, I love to twerk. I also have to keep my girl up on game, so she knows how to please her future husband.

"You so crazy," Bianca says, as she grabs her purse and heads out the door "Bye, girl!"

"Bye, Mrs. DeWayne." I say, as I close and lock the door.

I head back to my room to finished getting dressed. I hear my phone go off, alerting me that I have a DM from Instagram. I glance at my phone that's sitting on the nightstand, and my heart drops.

"Happy Valentine's Day, I just moved back in town and I was hoping I'd get to see you..."

I couldn't believe my eyes as I looked down at my phone seeing a DM from my ex, Keith.

"I thought I blocked him?" I mumbled to myself, with my face wrinkled in confusion.

As I looked at the message, all the emotions of the last day we spoke came back like a ton of bricks. I sat down on the bed and just stared at the phone, not knowing what to do next. The last time I spoke to Keith was three months ago. He told me he was moving and we couldn't be together. When I tried to plead my case that we could make it work, he never responded. A few weeks later, I see him on Instagram hugged up with someone else.

I picked up the phone and pressed reply to the message. My palms were sweaty and my thumbs began to move quickly.

> WTF?! So you just disappear for three months and now you want to see me? Tell me you want a future with me, but then leave and ignore me? Stomp on my heart like Columbus Short in Stomp the Yard, and now you're Dm'ing me like nothing happened? Oh hell no! I don't want to see you or hear from you EVER again.

I went to press send, but couldn't bring myself to do it. I deleted the message and just left it on "Seen". I grab my phone and walk into the kitchen to pour myself a drink. I lean against the counter with my leg crossed thinking about the first time we met. I try to hold back tears but I can't. I stand in the kitchen, tears staining my cheeks thinking about the love of my life...

CHAPTER 2

Lust Love at First Sight

I need one dance, got a Hennessey in my hand. One more time 'fore I go, higher powers taking a hold of me...

Music played in the background while I moved my hips to the beat of my jam *One Dance* by Drake. I could slow wind like Rihanna and all the chicks in the old Sean Paul videos. You couldn't tell me I wasn't an islander the way I moved my body like a snake. It was Friday night and the turn up was real. We were at one of the hottest spots in Atlanta, Café Circa, and it was packed on the rooftop. It was June so the weather was perfect for a little rooftop grinding. I was there with my girl, Mya, and it was always a story when her and I went out. She was my partner in crime. There was never a dull moment on an Arianna and Mya mission. We felt like the baddest chicks in the room by the amount of men who walked up to buy us drinks.

Mya stood 5'5", slim thick, with double D breasts. She had a gorgeous face with chinky eyes that she got from her Korean mother, and a booty she got from her African American side of the family. She had a short, black hair cut like Halle Berry in the nineties and men couldn't get enough of her. My girl was bad. I had known her since I was eighteen, but didn't get to see her much because she now lived in Los Angeles. But any time she came to the city, I knew it would be a good night.

"Girl, I think I'm gonna head to the bathroom after this song, that Ciroc is flowing through me." I said, still moving my hips to the beat.

"Okay girl, I'm going to chill right here and save our spot. I don't want any heffas trying to steal our table." Mya asserted, as she took a few steps back to sit down at the table we danced in front of.

"Don't hurt nobody!" I smiled, amused at how serious

Mya was about these seats. Once she was settled, I proceeded to the restroom.

As I made my way to the bathroom, I had to carefully squeeze through a crowd of people because there was barely any room to move. As I shuffled through the crowd, I tried my best to cover my butt from the creepy guys who would get really close to me just to cop a butt rub. Men could be such perverts sometimes. Like come on, keep your hands to yourself. After fighting my way through perves, I reached the restroom but there was a line. I took a deep breath trying to hold it in, and leaned against the wall to wait. I looked down to check myself to make sure I was still looking good. I had on my favorite high waist jeans that fit my curves just right, and a metallic gold crop top that drooped in the front and crisscrossed in the back. My hair was pulled up in a bun to show off my backless top and bring attention to my Georgia peach. I wore clear, strappy heels to bring the entire outfit together. I was looking good.

After checking myself out, I looked back up to see how far back I was in line. I had two people in front of me and it was almost my turn. I scanned the room while I waited, and that's when I saw him. There he stood, 6'6", chocolate, with a lean physique, like he may have played football at some point in time. He was rocking a pair of simple fitted jeans with a collared shirt that showed his impressive pecks, and retro Jordan's. We locked eyes and I found myself biting my bottom lip because this man was fine. He began to walk towards the bathroom. I hurried up and turned away because I didn't want to look like some stalker staring at this fine specimen of a man. I tried to play it off and act like I was looking ahead to wait for the bathroom.

"Excuse me, what's your name?" asked a deep, sexy voice from behind me.

I slowly turned around as my heart rate increased and my lady parts began to moisten.

"Uhh, I'm Arianna…"

He took my hand and shook it, then slowly leaned in and kissed me on the cheek.

"Nice to meet you, Arianna, I'm Keith."

"Oh shit, oh shit! Pull it together girl. You have to keep your cool in front of this piece of sexual chocolate. Do not faint! We have come too far. We need him in our life." I coached myself, as I processed what had just happened.

"Hellooo…are you just going to stand there, or are you going to use the restroom?" A chubby girl with a bad weave blurted out, interrupting my thought process. I was so caught up in the moment that I didn't realize it was my turn. If I wasn't so happy about Keith's fine self, I would've cussed Resputia out, but I let her live because I was on cloud nine after meeting him.

"Oh my bad. Keith, you mind waiting for me while I run to the lady's room real quick?" I batted my eyes persuasively, waiting for a response.

"Of course beautiful, take your time. I'll be right out here."

"Okay," I blushed, as I turned around to walk towards the restroom.

"About time, dang!" Mcfatty muttered as I opened the bathroom door.

I turned and gave her the "Bitch, I'll kill you" stare then proceeded into the restroom. I refused to let her steal my joy. I relieved myself, then I went to the mirror to make sure I was on point. I had to be flawless for that handsome man outside of that door. I reapplied my Ruby Woo Mac lipstick and I was ready to go. I exited the bathroom with butterflies still in my tummy. I looked up to see Keith still standing in the same spot I left him.

"You good sweetheart, you want a drink?" He offered, holding his hand out signifying that he wanted me to grab it. I grabbed his hand and allowed him to lead me towards the bar.

"Sure, why not?"

We made our way to the bar and I ordered my regular: A Ciroc Pineapple on the rocks. He ordered his drink and paid the bartender. As we waited for our drinks, he leaned down to speak to me so I could hear him over the music.

"So a Ciroc, no chaser huh? I'm scared of you." He looked down at me with those almond shaped eyes. I wanted to do him right there. I now knew what Usher meant in his hit record, "Love in This Club".

"I mean, I'm no light weight; I know how to handle myself." I gave sexy smirk looking up at Keith.

"Oh, you do, huh? Now if I have to carry you out the club, then you can't utter those words ever again." We both laughed.

The bartender then handed us our drinks, and he thanked her and handed her a ten-dollar tip. It's such a turn on to see a man who knows proper tipping etiquette.

"So, who are you here with?" Keith inquired as he took a sip of his drink.

"My girl, Mya" I pointed to where she was.

She looked to be preoccupied with a gentleman herself. I waved my hand to get her attention just in case she needed me to save her. She saw me waving and I motioned thumbs up, then thumbs down. She then gave me two thumbs up, and I grinned and shook my head yes. She then continued her conversation with the gentleman she was speaking to.

"She good," I assured him, taking a sip of my drink.

"Whoa, whoa, wait a minute. What was that? Some sort of girl code?" Keith smiled, showing his deep dimples and perfect white teeth. This man was about to be my baby daddy and he didn't even know it.

"Oh, for sure. I gave her thumbs up or down to see if she needed me to come save her. She then gave me two thumbs up to let me know she was good and I can stay where I am, and I shook my head yes to let her know I was in good hands too. I just gave you some top secret ish now, don't tell nobody."

We both started cracking up. I was glad he was enjoying my humor.

"I can tell you're hilarious. I like that. A woman who has a sense of humor is definitely a turn on." Keith looked directly into my eyes. I looked away and stared into my drink so he couldn't catch me blushing.

Work, work, work, work, work, work, work...Rihanna's hit *Work* blasted through the speaker.

"Oooohhhh, that's my jam!" I threw my hands in the air, moving my body to the beat of the song.

"Let me find out you got a little rhythm,"

"First of all, I got more than rhythm, I got skills. Second of all, you're about to find out sooner than you thought." I grabbed his hand and lifted it up and slow winded until I was right in front of him. I then turned around so my butt met his pelvis. I pulled his arm down and wrapped it around my waist.

"So, you still think I just got rhythm?" I purred, as I rolled my body down his slowly moving to the floor then winding back up.

Keith looked down speechless, his words caught in his throat "Uuuummmmm nah, you know exactly what you're doing." He responded, tightening his grip around my waist.

We danced for the next thirty minutes. It was absolutely perfect. It felt like we were in our own world and no one else was on the dancefloor but us. I didn't think this moment could get any better.

"Babe, you want another drink?"

"Yes babe, get me the same thing." I replied, still caught up in the song.

"I can't hear you."

I abruptly turned around and faced him. I stood on my tip toes and spoke into his ear so he could hear me better

"Yes babe, just get me the same thing." I repeated, as I lowered my body back down to the floor. But as I came down, something happened. It was like time slowed down and we locked eyes as my face came close to his. He stared at me and I stared back at him. Time literally stopped and we were the only people on Earth. Then, he kissed me. My lady parts were now on full flood, and I was trying not to pass out.

"Oh dang, I didn't mean to offend…" before he could utter another word, I placed both my hands on the back of his head and I kissed him back.

He wrapped his big, warm hands around my waist and held me close as we made out right by the bar like there was no one else there. I couldn't believe I was kissing a stranger in a club. Oh well, at least he was an attractive, seemingly nice stranger. We locked lips for about three minutes, then we both pulled apart from one another, still gazing into each other's eyes.

"So, you said you wanted the Ciroc Pineapple on the rocks right?" Keith teased, trying to deflect from our public make-out session.

"Boy, you're crazy," I shook my head yes, belly still full of butterflies at the thought of what had just occurred.

There was something unexplainable between us that neither of us could deny. He ordered our drinks and I just watched him in that moment. I didn't want the night to end. I didn't want to have to leave him. This was something I had never felt before and I wished I could press pause to stop time and live here forever.

"Hey girl! I'm about ready to go. You ready?" I heard Mya ask as she crept up behind me, interrupting my inner love thoughts of Keith.

"Uuuhhh, gimme one second and I'll be ready." I responded to Mya, my tone filled with uncertainty.

"Okay girl, I'll be over here when you're ready. You sure you're good?" Mya's face scrunched with concern.

"Great, actually," I grinned, not wanting Mya to know that I didn't want to leave, but I wanted to stay with Keith in that moment forever. "I'll come grab you in just a second, promise."

"Okay hon." She then walked back over to the table to take a seat and wait for me.

"You're about to leave me?" Keith inquired, as I turned back around to him and he met my glare with puppy dog eyes.

"Yes," I dropped my bottom lip displaying my disappointment.

"Baby, don't do that, you'll be seeing a lot more of me, I promise." Keith placed his finger underneath my chin, lifting my head so I looked right at him.

"You promise?" I held my pinky out so he could pinky swear promise me. I wasn't playing with him, he had to pinky swear so I knew it was real.

"I promise." He locked his pinky with mine to solidify

the promise. He then handed me his phone and I put my number in it. I gave it back and he placed it in his back pocket.

"I guess this is goodbye." I sighed.

"Nope, this is, see you later." he winked at me, leaning over to give me one final kiss for the evening.

I swear that kiss took my soul. This man had me sprung already and he didn't even know it. I blushed once more, then turned around and walked away. I got Mya's attention and motioned for her to meet me at the door. She got up from her seat and we headed downstairs to the front door. Once we got outside, Mya looked at me with her evil grin.

"BBBIIITTTCCCHHHH! Did I see you kissing that fine ass guy at the bar?!" Mya gushed, as we walked down the street headed to our Uber.

I looked in the air blushing, taking a deep breath before responding "YYYAAASSSS BITCH!!! I think I'm in love, girl!" I stopped and looked at Mya with a huge smile.

"Girl, stop! You're in lust. You've only known him for five minutes. He is fine though, so I can see how you'd get that confused."

"Nah bruh, this is love, or something like it. I ain't neva felt a connection like that with someone. And you know I don't be just kissing negros in the club! I got an image to uphold."

"Okay, girl! Well, excuse me. Get yo groove back then, Stella." Mya smirked, while she did a little wind to emphasize me getting my groove back.

"Shut up, crazy," I giggled, "But girl seriously! I didn't wanna leave, but I didn't wanna seem too pressed and I also didn't wanna keep you waiting. I could've stayed there with that man all night, girl! Like, I'm legit trippin' right now!"

"Well girl, the night is still young, who knows what could transpire? Where the hell is this Uber?" Mya asked, her voice filled with irritation as she looked up and down the block.

"Arianna! Wait up!" I heard a voice yell from behind me. I quickly turned around to see who it was, and it instantly put a huge smile on my face. It was Keith, jogging down the block to catch up to me.

"Man, I had to leave because it was pointless to be there without you." Keith said, his voice soft with affection. He looked down at me smiling, with those sexy ass dimples.

"You know you need to stop. You left because you wanted to, not because of me."

"Nah, forreal. There ain't nothing up there for me. I'm about to ride out. I'm gonna hit you up real soon." Keith assured, as he leaned in and kissed me once more.

"Okay, I will try not to hold my breath." I stated sarcastically, smiling from ear to ear as I saw him walk to his car.

"Well damn. bitch! Maybe it is love!" Mya exclaimed, with a shocked look on her face after watching our interaction.

"Told you biiihhhhh!" I playfully dougied down the block. We both bust out laughing.

My phone alerted me that my Uber had finally arrived. We got in the car and headed back to my place. On the ride home I just zoned out thinking about Keith the entire time. We didn't get to talk much in the club, so there was so much more I wanted to know about him. I was so engulfed in my thoughts I didn't even realize we had made it home already.

"Earth to Arianna, get out the car crazy!" Mya nudged me to get my attention.

"Girl, I'm sorry, I'm so zoned out." I responded, as I reached to open the door.

"Thank you!" I yelled at the Uber driver, as he drove away.

"Well, I'm about to head to one of my boo thangs house. I'll text you when I get there." Mya admitted, as she walked towards her rental car.

"Wayment, how you got boos in Atlanta. You live in LA?" I interrogated, with a curious look on my face.

"Now you know I got hoes in different area codes. Keep up chick." Mya rubbed her hands together with a mischievous grin.

I just laughed and shook my head "You a mess. Don't do anything I wouldn't do." I shouted, as I headed into my townhouse.

"Well that means I can do errthang I was thinking and more."

"Whateva heffa!" I retorted, waving at her as I watched her drive away.

I went into my house and locked the door. I took my shoes off and put my purse on the counter and headed to the kitchen. Why is it 2:30AM? We were not supposed to be out this late. And I'm hungry. I know there isn't anything in here to eat. Ugh, this is aggravating. I heard my phone vibrating in my purse. I ran to see who it was in hopes that nothing had happened to Mya. I saw a number I didn't recognize. It was too late to be a telemarketer, so I answered.

"Hello, who's this?" my voice filled with annoyance.

"Is that how you answer the phone for the future father of your kids? Sheesh!"

"Keith? I didn't know who this was," I chuckled. "What you want?"

"To see you right now."

"Uh uh. Momma said ain't nothing open but legs and Waffle House at this hour." I challenged, in my no nonsense tone.

"Exactly, so meet me at Waffle House by Georgia State downtown." Keith requested sternly, like he wasn't going to take no for an answer.

I waited a second as I thought about it, and then responded "Aight, gimme a few minutes to put on something comfortable."

"Okay, but don't keep me waiting too long. You know

I miss you already." Keith was dripping all his sauce on this conversation and I was eating it up. But I couldn't let him know that.

"Bye, boy. I'll see you in a second."

I threw on a black, Pink sweat suit and black, low top vans. I touched up my makeup so I could look chill cute, but not like I tried too hard. I headed to Waffle House with butterflies in my tummy, excited to see Keith. When I pulled up, it was packed and I took my phone out to see if he had arrived yet. As soon as I was about to send the text, I felt a hand grab mines. I turned around abruptly, thinking I was going to have to smack somebody, but then realized it was him.

"Right this way, my lady." Keith said, as he led me to a table in the back.

"Boy, don't walk up on me like that. You almost got molly whopped."

He turned around and looked at me unconvinced, "Girl, you don't even know what that means."

"I grew up in College Park, don't try it." I shot him a stare to let him know I meant business.

"Well, knuck if you buck then!" Keith squared up

playfully like he was about to fight me.

I bust out laughing and pushed him out of his stance. "You're a nut." We both laughed then sat down once we got to our table.

We looked over the menus and placed our orders. After we got our food, we dove into a deep conversation. We talked about our future, marriage, how many kids we wanted, our backgrounds, and everything we could think of. When we finally looked up, the sun was rising and it was 6:30AM. This night would certainly go down for one of the best nights of my life.

"OMG, I can't believe it's 6:30AM! How did this happen?" I asked rhetorically.

"They say time flies when you're having fun."

BBBZZZZZ BBBBZZZZZ

I looked down at my phone to see Marbles calling and it snapped me out of my daydream.

"Shit! I'm not even dressed yet!" I panicked, knowing he was calling to pick me up for our Valentine's Day lunch. I answered the phone.

"Hey sexy, you ready?" I was instantly turned off. "Why did I agree to this?" I thought to myself.

"Not yet, but give me a few minutes and I'll be outside."
I said in an frustrated tone before hanging up the phone.
This was going to be a horrible date.

CHAPTER 3

Baby Momma Drama at Benihana

"Happy Valentine's Day! You guys make a lovely couple. Can I start you off with something to drink?" the Benihana waitress greeted us.

"Can I have a shot of tequila please? Nope, make that a double shot." I requested, my voice filled with desperation. "Make that pronto if you can."

"Dang girl, slow down. We just got here." Marbles said naively ignoring my displeased demeanor.

I gave him a death stare as he looked at the menu then a redirected my attention to the waitress. "Ma'am, can I please get my drink like asap?"

Reading my look of despair, the waitress responded. "Yes ma'am, a double shot of tequila coming right up. Sir, I'll bring you both waters while you decide."

"Thank you so much," I replied graciously, placing my hands together letting her know how much I appreciated her for recognizing to my cry for help.

I had only been with Marbles for thirty minutes, and he was already working on my last nerve. I spent the entire ride listening to him go on and on about the celebrities he was working with, and how he's securing the bag. I felt like I was listening to a DJ Khaled snap. This negro hadn't asked me how I was doing, or how my day was going. He was too busy gassing himself up the entire time, and telling me about all the money he was making. You know what I never understood? Why men brag about how much money they have then get mad when they attract gold diggers? If you lead with money, women who want that money will follow.

But I had no idea why he was telling me this stuff, I couldn't care less. I had my own money, and he couldn't do a thing for me. I met Marbles on Instagram. I had been peeping him for a while because he was extra cute. He was pretty popular in the city because he produced for a lot of hot artists. I didn't care about his status though, I just wanted to see what that D did because he was so aesthetically pleasing. Well we never quite got around to that because every time I got around him, I felt like I was being tortured by stupidity. Each time I left I told myself I would never do it again, but he just always knew when to contact me. It's like he had some kind of sensor that let him know when I was desperate so it was time to text me. Bianca was right about this, I shouldn't have stooped this low. I have to figure out how to get out of here. I don't know if I can make it through an entire lunch with this fool.

"What you thinking 'bout getting, with yo' sexy ass?" Marbles asked, looking like he was undressing me with his eyes.

I gave him a fake giggle and put my face in the menu so I could roll my eyes in peace. "I think I'm going to do the Lunch Duet with filet mignon and scallops."

"Filet mignon is that pasta stuff right? Yea, I got that last time I was here."

I take a deep sigh with my face planted in the menu. I look up to the sky and ask God why me, then I respond to his ignorance. "Actually, it's a steak."

"Girl, I knew that, I was just joking, you so uptight."

I didn't know if he was kidding or not, but I really didn't care. I just wanted the waitress to bring the double shot to calm my nerves.

"Tyrek," I hear a female's voice yell from across the restaurant.

"That's his name." I whispered to myself. I had been calling him Marbles for so long that I had forgotten his actual name.

"Tyrek! I know you hear me," hollers a strange woman that is briskly approaching our table.

Tyrek looks up like he had seen a ghost. "Latoya, what the hell are you doing here?" Tyrek says, his voice filled with guilt.

"I should be asking you that! You told me you were going to LA to work with an artist. But here you are, still in Atlanta at our favorite restaurant." The woman yelled, as she leaned to the side with her hand steadily placed on her left hip while rolling her neck around with every word.

"See what had happened was, the trip had um..." Tyrek fumbled over his words, trying to think of a feasible lie for his current predicament.

"Uh uh negro, you ain't bout to lie out of this one" Latoya screeched, cutting Marbles off before he could even finish the sentence. "And who is this Tyrek?" She swiftly pointed her finger at me.

I was so entertained by the madness that was unfolding in front of me that I forgot that I was sitting in the midst of this Jerry Springer episode. I just hope she isn't one of those chicks who tries to fight the innocent bystander because I have no idea who she is. I don't even care about this guy. I'm just here for the free food. I snapped back to my reality and responded.

"Oh hey girl, my name is Arianna." I stretched my hand out to introduce myself.

There was a brief pause as Latoya stared at my hand deciding her next move, as Marbles gazed blankly trying to figure out how he would get out of this situation.

"Arianna huh? Well, did you know that the man

you're sitting with has two kids by me and another one on the way? Yes, I'm two months pregnant." Latoya revealed, dropping a bomb on the entire restaurant. By now, everyone in the Benihana was watching this soap opera unfold.

I coughed, choking a little after hearing what she had just exposed. "Say what now? Mar...I mean Tyrek; you have a whole baby on the way? Plus two kids? You told me you only had one and you said your baby mother lived in another state and-"

"Another state?!" Latoya interrupted. "Girl stop, I live with his punk ass. We've been together for eight years. You're not the first ho and you probably won't be the last, but he's mines boo boo."

Did she just call me out my name? You know what, I'm not even about to start with her because she's pregnant and her hormones are high. Plus, I don't want Marbles, so I'm not about to engage in this nonsense because it's obvious she's ratchet and may fight me. I'm too cute to be fighting, and I love Benihana. I refuse to let baby momma get me banned from one of my favorite restaurants.

I got up from my seat and grabbed my purse. "You know what Latoya, you are absolutely right. He is yours, and I don't want to stand between your love any longer. I'm going to catch this Uber and be out of y'all way. Congrats on the baby sis." I got up from the table and scurried away from the drama I was just consumed in.

I still heard Latoya calling Marbles everything but a son of God, but that was no longer my business. I would be blocking his number because I don't have time for the bull. One thing I'm not is a side chick. Forget being number one, I have to be the only one. I'm not fighting for no man's attention. Especially after eight years. But to each his own. I can't judge Latoya because we have all been someone's fool at some point in time. I ordered my Uber and made my way home. I couldn't wait to tell Bianca about the drama that had just transpired.

* * *

"Hey, you can just drop me off right here by the mailbox?" I instructed my Uber driver after we entered the gates to my complex.

He did as he was told and dropped me off right in front of the community mailboxes. I thanked him as I closed the door and got out of the car. I rarely ever checked my mail, but I might as well seeing that I had nothing else to do on this horrible day. It was only 5PM and still Valentine's Day. I guess I'd spend the rest of my day drinking wine, watching Waiting to Exhale, and sulking in my misery. I keep telling Bianca I'm cursed, I don't know why she doesn't believe me. Maybe she'll be more convinced after I share this story with her.

"Bills, bills, and more bills. You think they'd say Happy V Day or something to at least motivate me to want to pay this crap." I mumbled, realizing the reason why I never checked my mail. There was nothing but bills and irrelevant promotions. This wasn't making my day any better.

"Hey, you dropped this." a male voice stated from behind me.

I turned around to see who it was and my lady parts

began to tingle at the sight of him. There stood a rich chocolate brother that looked like he could be on the cover of GQ. He was 6'2", the physique of a male model, light brown eyes, with nice full lips I wanted to bite. He had that Tyson Beckford swag and I was caught all up in it.

"Hey, you okay?" the fine mystery man questioned, snapping me out of my nasty thoughts.

"Oh yea, what did you say, I'm sorry."

"I said you dropped your mail." he stated, as he handed me a Victoria Secret coupon.

"Oh, thanks. I could definitely use this after the day I'm having."

"Valentine's Day woes?" the mystery man inquired.

"Man, you don't even know the half, but I'll be okay after this wine and movie. I'm surprised you even know what today is. Most men block it out of their psyche, unless you're married or have a girlfriend."

He laughed "No, I'm not married or in relationship, but my mother's birthday just happens to be today so I always remember."

"Oh wow, today is her birthday? That has to suck. She only gets one gift even though this counts as two holidays for her."

"Well, my father goes all out for her birthday, so she doesn't have it too bad. He surprised her with a trip to Jamaica last night. They left on a flight this morning." His face lit up at the thought of how well his dad treats his mom.

"Yasss! Yo' daddy better set the bar high!" I rejoiced, snapping my finger in the air.

He laughed at my hand snapping, "Yea, he is good to my mom. He definitely gives me something to look up to."

There was a moment of silence, and we both looked into each other's eyes. I'm not sure what he was thinking, but I was picturing our future home and what our babies would look like. We had a connection and I knew he felt it.

"So what's your name?" he asked, breaking the awkward moment.

"I'm Arianna, what yours?"

"I'm Maurice, but my friends call me Mo."

"How about this, Arianna? Instead of spending the rest of your evening watching depressing movies, how about you spend it with me at dinner, tonight. That is if your boyfriend won't get mad and try to beat me up."

"First of all, *Waiting to Exhale* isn't depressing, it's a classic. It's actually quite empowering. Second of all, I'm single. Third of all, what time are you picking me up?" I smirked, excited that he was asking me on a date.

"Alright, it is a classic. You're reaching with the empowering part though, but I'll let you have it. I'll pick you up at 7PM. How does that sound?"

"That's sounds perfect, Mr. Maurice."

"Well, let me get your number so I can hit you up when I'm headed your way." Mo handed me his phone.

"How about I just give you my apartment number. If the date goes well, you can get my number. If not, we can avoid the awkward postdate texts trying to see if we like each other or not and tonight can just be the end of it." I typed in my apartment information and handed him his phone back.

"Oh okay, that's how you want to play it then, Ms. Arianna? Cool, challenge accepted." Mo took his phone, nodding his head agreeing to my terms.

"You just better be on time, Mr. I'll see you tonight." I winked at him as I turned around and walked away.

"Oh, I'll be right on time." Mo muttered while he

watched the amazing view of me from behind.

I made my way back to my townhouse on cloud nine. Although I had a horrible lunch date with Marbles, I had just gotten invited to dinner by a sexy piece of man candy. Maybe I wasn't cursed after all. I just knew I had to look like a whole snack for my date tonight. This man was fine and it seemed like he knew how to treat a lady. I had to get him on my team. As I approached my door, I could see a balloon and flowers sitting outside. I had no idea who could've sent that. I hope it wasn't Marbles who dropped it off. I doubt it because I'm sure he was still at Benihana getting cussed out by his baby momma. I got to my door and grabbed the card out of the bouquet of sunflowers which were my favorite. They must've spent a pretty penny because sunflowers weren't in season.

```
Please have dinner with me. I'm sorry
and I really miss you
Keith
```

So now you want to have dinner? You didn't want to have dinner four months ago when I pleaded for you to talk to me. Men are so funny to me sometimes. When you're in one hundred percent, they take you for granted and treat you like gum on the bottom of their shoes. But as soon as you remove yourself from the situation, that's when they want to come running back. It was like a never ending cycle. I wasn't about to play this cat and mouse game with Keith. I can't lie and say I didn't miss him. He was the love of my life and I would probably always love him, but I just refuse to continue to let him break my heart. You know how the old saying goes, fool me once, shame on you, fool me twice, shame on me. I picked the flowers up and carried them in placing them on the counter. I wasn't going to waste good sunflowers just because Keith was a butthole. I then proceeded to my room to get dressed for my hot date.

"Tonight will be a good night." I told myself, as I opened my closet and rummaged through my clothes. I grabbed my phone and played Sabrina Claudio's *Unravel Me*. I sang along as I readjusted my focus on tonight. I refused to let Keith unravel me.

"I know you're trying, but you'll never unravel me…"

CHAPTER 4

I Want Some Mo

Knock knock knock

"Dang, it's 7PM already!" I thought, rushing through the house trying to put the finishing touches on my ensemble.

I had to be seductively sexy, but still classy for my first date with Mo. He had really caught my eye and I wanted to impress him. I didn't know where we were going, but a little black dress fits every occasion. I made sure I did my makeup just enough that it stood out, but still looked natural. I wand curled my twenty-two inch Brazilian wavy bundles to get that Angela Simmons curl. That girl's hair stays laid. It was a little chilly so I paired my black dress with my open toe lace booties from Steve Madden. They made my calves sit up just right. I grabbed my cropped leather jacket from Express, and made sure my red lipstick was perfect. I completed my getup with Black Angel perfume from Victoria Secret. I was looking good, but smelling even better.

"Coming!" I yelled, as I slowly jogged to the door.

I opened the door to see Mo standing there looking like a whole snack. He wore dark, stone washed jeans with a burgundy sweater that showed his peck imprints perfectly. He paired it with cognac colored combat boots, and a black pea coat to pull it all together. There is nothing like a man in a pea coat that knows how to wear it right, such a turn on. This man was not only sexy, but he could dress his ass off too. I think we have a winner.

"You look," he paused, taking me all in, "stunning." Keith complimented, taking my hand into his while looking me up and down.

Yea, I looked good and I knew it. "Why thank you. You don't look half bad yourself." I teased.

Moe grinned as he led me out of my house and to his car. We walked to a black on black Mercedes CLS coupe with tinted windows. When he opened the door for me, I noticed his custom red seats with gold M's embedded in them.

"Okay then." I murmured, as I waited for him to walk around and get in the car.

He opened the door and sat down putting his seatbelt on and cranking the car. "Are you good madam? Would you like for me to turn the heater on or the seat warmer?"

"The heat yes, but no to the seat warmer. Look at you with your fancy car. You got moneeeyyyyyyy." I joked.

Mo laughed, "Girl, you crazy."

We pulled out of my complex and headed towards the city. "So, where are we headed?" I pried.

"Just sit back and relax nosey, I got this."

I love it when a man takes charge. I bit my bottom lip and crossed my legs trying to control my juices from flowing. This man had everything I needed so I had to keep my lady parts all the way in check.

"Okay, okay, I'll let you lead. This yo world, I'm just in it for the evening."

"Exactly beautiful. So, sit back and relax, and I'm going to show you a night you'll never forget. Just trust me." Moe winked at me and I melted.

"Well, can we at least turn on some music and set the mood. Let me connect my phone to your Bluetooth cuz my playlist is bangin." I reached for his digital radio.

"Uh uh! Chris Tucker told you to neva touch a black man's radio." Mo smacked my hand playfully. "I got this girl, I know my playlist is better than yours."

"Oh really now? What you got, huh?"

I leaned back waiting to see what he was going to play. Then 6lack *Learn Ya* came bumping out of the stereo.

"What you know 'bout that, young man? 6lack is my guy!" I confidently proclaimed. I bobbed my head to the music and sang along to the song.

"Oh, so you're a 6lack fan, huh? I guess that's our first thing in common." Moe looked over at me while I zoned out, vibing to the music.

"Yaassss! He has, like the greatest bitter negro breakup album of all time."

"Not bitter breakup album." Moe grinned, "You something else. I can tell it's never a dull moment with you."

"Oh, you ain't seen nothing yet." I looked at Mo with a mischievous grin. We both laughed and he just shook his head. We vibed out to the 6lack album for the remainder of the ride.

We were headed towards the midtown area and I was trying to guess where he could possibly be taking me. I knew it would be fancy because we were on Peachtree. I was hoping there wouldn't be a wait wherever we were going because I was starving. I knew Valentine's Day would have all the restaurants packed, but I was praying he had a reservation. We finally pulled up to a place and stopped for valet. I was pleasantly surprised when I saw the sign to STK. I had been to this restaurant before and it wasn't cheap.

"Good evening, Mr. Lewis, you want us to park it in your usual spot?" the valet greeted Mo and opened his door, while another gentleman came to my side to open my door.

"Yes sir, Alan, thank you." Mo said, as he got out of the car and handed the valet guy a tip. He walked around to my side and took my hand.

"Shall we?" He led me into the restaurant.

For some reason, I had so many butterflies in my stomach. When we met at the mailbox, I just thought he was some fine nice guy who lived in my neighborhood. Now that I am here with him, he seems like a big deal. This made me even more nervous and I felt even more inclined to make a perfect first impression. I needed to calm down. Deep breath Arianna, you got this.

"Hi, Mr. Lewis, we have your table set up in the back. Amanda will take you to it." A man in a black suit advised Moe.

I assumed he was the manager by his well-groomed appearance. A Caucasian young woman grabbed two menus and we followed her through the restaurant. It was packed out for Valentine's Day. By the look of the foyer, they were booked all night because there were a few dozen people waiting to be seated. I was geeked we weren't one of them because I was too hungry for that type of waiting. We went all the way to the back of the restaurant and we ended up at a sliding door. It looked like it led to a private area. The young lady slid the doors back and I was in awe.

"Here you are Mr. Lewis, your waiter will be right with you." the hostess said as she walked away leaving us in private.

I stood there with my mouth open taking in the décor. The room was small, but so beautiful. It had dark brick paneling with an antique wood table in the center. There was a huge rustic colored, wine cabinet that took up most of the room, but it went perfectly with the ambiance. The room was dimly lit with candles illuminating from the center. I looked down to see a bouquet of roses with a teddy bear on one end of the table. I was still standing there with my mouth open trying to figure out if this was my reality, or if I was dreaming.

"So, you want to sit down and eat gorgeous, or you prefer standing? Either way is cool with me." Mo wittily inquired, as he grabbed my hand and led me to the seat.

"My bad, I was just trying to figure out if this was reality, or was I on an episode of Power and you're James St. Patrick." I joked. "But seriously, how'd you pull all this together in such a short amount of time?"

In my mind, I thought he must've had a date with someone else and something happened and I was just a rebound. I'd never say that out loud because you never want the man you're with to be thinking of anyone but you. Also, I didn't care if I was a rebound at this point. I was just ready to have the bomb.com evening.

"I made a few phone calls. I host a lot of my clients here so they kind of like me." Mo responded modestly.

"Clients? Oh lawd, please don't tell me you're on your Ghost stuff forreal! I was just kidding, but if that's what you're into I'm not trying to be a ride or die chick. I'm too cute for jail." I began to look over my shoulders because I suddenly felt like someone was watching me.

"Nooooo," Mo bust out laughing, "I'm far from a drug dealer."

I let out a sigh of relief and felt safe again.

"I'm an investor. I teach my clients how to properly invest their money so they don't end up broke. Most of my clients are black wealthy men who don't want banks touching their money, so they come to me so I can teach them how to properly invest without a middle man."

My face lit up, I was highly impressed. "Wow, now that's amazing. I have my own tax business. I teach individuals what taxes actually are and how not to get caught up with the IRS. My clients are mostly black people as well because our community knows nothing about taxes. All they know is W-2s and having kids equals big bucks on their tax return. They know nothing beyond that point."

Mo started nodding his head up and down.

"Why are you nodding your head?" I giggled.

"Because I knew I wanted you because of your vibe, and your beauty added to that. But now I know I have to have you after hearing that you have brains to go along with all that."

My whole face turned red from blushing.

"Chill, I'm just trying to help my community just like you." I put my head down so he wouldn't see how red my face was.

He reached over the table and grabbed my hand and kissed it. I looked up to see Mo staring at me.

"Well, maybe we could be a team and help the community together."

At this point, I was going to need to change my underwear because it was an ocean down there. We just looked at one another, wanting each other right then and there.

"Good evening, Mr. Lewis and his lovely date. Can I start you guys off with something to drink?" The waiter came in and broke the sexual tension in the room.

Thank God because I didn't have time to be on WorldStar for being caught sexing on the first date in the back of STK. Mo ordered a bottle of champagne and asked if I wanted anything else. What I wanted wasn't on the menu, so I told him that was fine. The waiter went to get the drink orders and we picked back up on our career conversation.

What started off as a conversation about our similar career paths ended in us learning everything about one another. Mo told me about how he grew up in a two parent household and his father taught him how to properly treat a woman. He said although he knew he was a good catch, he had trouble dating because he didn't date how society expected him to date. He didn't juggle several women, and he always put all of his eggs in one basket. That had gotten him heartbroken a few times because he soon found out that most Atlanta women had several men at once. He also said it was hard weeding out who actually wanted him versus who just wanted his status and money. I was shocked to hear a man this fine and this great of a catch struggled in dating. It's crazy how we always think we struggle alone but we actually don't.

I told him how I grew up in a single parent household, and my mom had never been married. It had always been rough dating for me because I never had that father figure, so I had to validate myself. I explained how I had bumped my head several times because I seemed to attract every fuck boy in America. I briefly told him about Keith and how that was my last serious situation. I even told him about the earlier situation with Marbles. He died laughing and didn't believe me.

"I can't make this stuff up. Latoya said she was pregnant and he was her man." We both cackled until we cried. It was way funnier in retrospect than it was when I was actually in it.

"Here's your check, you guys have a lovely evening." The waitress dropped the check on the table, but before she could walk out, Mo handed her his card.

I looked down at my phone "Sheesh, it's 10:30 already! Time does fly when you're having fun."

"10:30 is early. The night is still young, and I still got a few tricks up my sleeve."

"Oh really, well I should've ordered a Red Bull cuz it's close to my bedtime, and I don't know if I can hang." I yawned.

"You'll be aight."

The waitress came back with Mo's card and he signed it. We got up to leave the restaurant. When we walked to the front it was almost empty. We had closed STK down. We got in his car and Mo headed north on Peachtree. I wondered where he was taking me. Dinner was way more than enough, and he had even more up his sleeve. If he was taking me to a wedding chapel to get hitched, I was ready to say yes. I know that was far-fetched, but with how perfect my night was going, it was possible. We pulled up to a gray, one leveled building that had no signs out front. There were several fancy cars in the parking lot, including an orange Lamborghini and a black Bentley coupe. He parked then got out to come open the door for me.

"You not taking me in to sell me off to some trafficking ring are you? This building looks super sketchy." I stepped out the car a little nervous and unaware of my surroundings.

"Girl, relax, nobody is going to kidnap you or sell you." Mo ensured me as he grabbed my hand and led me to the door.

He knocked twice and the door opened.

"Whaddup Mo!" A really tall and muscular guy opened the door and dapped Mo up.

I assumed he was a security guard because he wore all black and looked like he could whoop some ass. He opened the door and let us both in.

"How you doing, Ms.Lady?" the security guard acknowledged me as I walked in.

"I'm great, Happy Valentine's Day." I said to the security guard.

"Same to you," he responded, as he checked me out while Mo walked in front of me. Men were so bold. They didn't care who you were with, they just had to sneak a peek. I rolled my eyes and kept walking.

We proceeded to the back of the building and I started to hear people talking and soft music playing. When we got to the back it was a huge studio space with a band set up and a mic. There were about thirty people in the room and I recognized many faces from TV. Bambi and Scrappy from Love and Hip Hop were there, as well as 2 Chainz along with his wife, plus T.I. and Tiny. I was so geeked on the inside, but I had to hold my composure and act like I had been somewhere.

"Whaddup Mo!" 2 Chainz walked up and dapped Mo. "I see you got a beautiful lady witcha. I neva see you wit nobody, I was starting to think you played for the other team." He teased.

"Nigga, now you know that ain't neva been true and neva will be true." Mo retorted.

"Trruuuuueeeeee," 2 Chainz busted out his famous ad lib.

We all just laughed.

"I'll holla at cha later boy. I'm about to go kick back and watch my boy 6lack do his thang." 2 Chainz said, as he walked back to sit next to his wife.

"So, when you said wealthy black men, I didn't know you meant 2 Chainz. I love him!" I playfully nudged Mo for holding back that his clients were celebrities.

"I try not to boast about that stuff. I don't want people to think I'm bragging you know?"

"Oh, I totally understand that. And did he say 6lack was performing. Is that why the stage is set up?" I looked at Mo curiously.

"Yep, you heard right. I was testing you in the car to see if you even knew who he was. That was going to determine if I brought you here tonight. A few of my homies set this up to have a romantic evening with their ladies and I thought you might enjoy it." Mo smiled at me and pinched my chin softly.

I tried to hold back my excitement, but I was smiling ear to ear. "Well, I'm so happy I passed the test."

Mo grabbed my hand and led me to our seats. Once I sat down he went and grabbed us two glasses of champagne. As soon as he took his seat, 6lack walked out and began his set. We sat there grooving to each song singing all the words. Mo took my hand in his and looked at me.

"You good baby?"

"Oh I'm great, boo." I looked at him reassuringly.

I scooted closer to him, allowing him to wrap his arm around my waist as I rested my head on his shoulder. In that moment, I felt safe. I felt I could lay in his arms forever. This man barely knew me, but by his actions tonight, I felt like he really wanted more than just something physical. He wanted all of me and I wanted to give it to him. And not on a physical level, this was way deeper than that. I sat there wondering if he was the reason it didn't work out with anyone else. I embraced the thought of him being my forever. But at that moment, all I could do was live in it. This would go down as one of the best nights of my life.

CHAPTER 5

Who Got Some Cuddy Last Night?

"So the real question is, did you get some cuddy that night?" Bianca asked in suspense.

"Girl, no! I'm a lady; I don't give it up that quick, sheesh!" I dramatically placed my hand on my chest, clutching my imaginary pearls. "After the listening party, he brought me home and we sat in the car and talked for like two hours. He then kissed me on the forehead, and we parted ways." I gushed, reminiscing on my first date with Mo. It had been a month since Valentine's Day, and we were going strong.

"The forehead kiss is real! I'm glad you kept your panties on after that. That forehead kiss is a panty dropper."

"Girl, you ain't neva lied! I was wetter than Niagara Falls, but I couldn't let him know that. I want a future with him, can't be out here giving him the goodies that quickly."

"Amen!" We high-fived in agreeance to keeping the cookie in the cookie jar.

When you really like a man, it is necessary to hold out on sex until you figure out what his intentions are. It's not a game, it is for protection. You're protecting your heart because what if he ends up being a fuck boy? It's also for his protection because if he does end up being a fuck boy, you'll be obligated to fuck him up. It's a win/win situation.

"But girl, he is an amazing man. We communicate all day, every day. He is the first person I speak to in the morning, and the last person I speak to at night. He's so different from my past you know. He really seems to be all in." I stared at the ceiling, smiling as I spoke about Mo. I really cared about him.

"You know I love you, right?" B looked at me.

I sighed, knowing where this was going. "You love

me, but…" I looked back at B, waiting for her to kill my vibe.

"But you've only known him for a month. He's great and all, but allow him to prove that he's really going to stick around before investing your all. You know I love you and really want to see you happy with a great guy, but don't be too eager."

I rolled my eyes "Uuuggghhh, must we do this every time I meet someone?"

"Arianna, don't do that, you know I only want what's best for you. I hate seeing you hurt, and I've seen this too many times. You meet a guy, he's Prince Charming in the beginning, you invest your all super-fast, then he ends up being an extreme f boy, and I'm trying to figure out how I can kill this fool and hide the body sufficiently."

"But Mo is different though, he wants what I want." I expressed innocently.

"But you felt the same way about Keith, Devantae, oh and let's never forget Fat Devil."

I quickly shot a look of death towards Bianca. "We don't speak about Fat Devil in my home."

B held her hands up and leaned back "My bad, but I had to bring him up to prove a point. Won't happen again, don't shoot me."

"Cool, I'm glad we understand each other." We stared at one another for a moment then bust out laughing.

"You know I hate Fat Devil and everything he stands for! I can't believe I had to take that fool to court for my money. How you lie and say your mom died not to pay me?! WHO DOES THAT?!" I ranted, thinking about a horrible human being I used to date. "But anyway, I hear what you're saying. I know I need to be careful and I plan to. That's why I haven't given him the punaney, yet. I'm trying to be careful, like forreal."

Bianca scrunched her face skeptically, "Alright. I'm gonna take your word for it, but I hope I don't have to catch a case for setting his fancy car on fire. You know I love fire?"

I shook my head up and down, "Yes, I know you love fire. I hope I don't have to bail you out. Can't have my brother-in-law mad at me." I giggled.

"So, are you seeing him tonight?"

"Yep. He's coming over for the first time. I'm about to whip up my mantrap dinner."

"Whaatttt?! You are not about to put him on the collard greens and country style ribs with the skillet cornbread?" B leaned back in shock.

"And you know this!" I said, clapping at each word.

My momma didn't raise no woman who didn't know her way around the kitchen. Being from Mississippi, I knew how to throw down. Many women felt like the way to a man's heart nowadays was good nookie, but I knew the truth. Good nookie may bring him to your door, but good food would keep him coming back for more.

"You're trying to steal this man soul and put him in the sunken place."

"And neva let him out!" We both cracked up.

"Well, let me get out of here and let you get your Aunt Jemima on." Bianca got up from the couch where she was sitting, and headed towards the door.

"Okay, girl. Enjoy your day, but don't let it be another month before I see you. I need my girl time." I headed towards the door to give B a hug goodbye.

"You're right, but this wedding planning got me all

out of whack. My bad girl."

"It's cool, I get it. Planning your bachelorette party has been intense, so I know the wedding planning is crazy. But you already know we getting litty!" I said while doing the tootsie roll.

"Bye with your crazy self." B snickered as she walked out the door.

I went to the kitchen to prepare my grocery list. I wanted to make sure everything was perfect for my dinner with Mo tonight. I didn't want to screw this up. As I prepared my list, I couldn't help but contemplate on the conversation Bianca and I had just had. Was I moving too fast? To me I was moving at a good pace because I was following Mo's lead, but I did the same thing with Keith and we see how that turned out. I couldn't allow this to turn into another situation like that, but I didn't want to put a block on my emotions and make Mo pay for what Keith had done. Ugh, I don't want to overthink this. Let me just see how tonight goes and take it from there. I know I've said it before, but I really do believe Mo is different, I just hope he proves me right.

* * *

Knock-knock-kncok

7 o-clock on the dot, and Mo was at my door. I love how punctual this man is. He was always five minutes early, or right on time.

"Coming!" I yelled, as I sashayed to the door.

I was so excited for Mo to be coming to my place for the first time. He had picked me up several times and knew exactly where I lived but he had never been inside. I made sure I cleaned my place from top to bottom. No man liked a nasty woman, so I had to show him I knew how to keep a house in order. I made sure to boil some Fabuloso, so he knew it was real. I broke out my Caramel Pumpkin Bath & Body Works candle, so it smelled real sweet and sultry. I also wanted this to be a moment where he saw me in my everyday natural state. I knew how to slay with the best of them and I love a stiletto and a thigh high boot, but most of the times, I was on my "sweat pants hair tied chilling with no makeup on" flow. I wanted the effortlessly cute look. So I went with my black Forever 21 tights with an oversized Pink shirt that drooped over the shoulder. I had a fresh face, but I made sure my eyebrows were poppin'. Eyebrows could take a basic chick to a dime, so they were very important. I had my toes freshly pedicured with a tangerine color, and my hair in a messy bun. I was ready to steal his soul.

"Hey baby, welcome to my humble abode." I said to Mo, as I opened the door and spread out my right hand to welcome him in.

He stopped and looked at me up and down. "Damn."

"What?" I looked down at myself, confused as to why he was looking at me like that.

"You look amazing. Any woman can be stunning with heels and makeup, but you're not even trying and you look like this. Come here." Mo grabbed my hand, and pulled me in for a hug. I embraced him. He always smelled so good, such a turn on. I had to let go because I could already feel myself getting in the mood. I had to keep the cookie in the cookie jar. He let go, and kissed me gently with his soft lips. I almost melted in the doorway, but I had to pull it together.

"Don't be acting like you miss me." I teased as I pulled

Mo's hand and guided him through the door.

"Mmmm, mmm, mmm! It smells good in here! Let me find out you can cook." Mo took a deep breath to take in the aroma of collard greens, cornbread, and baked ribs. It smelled like Sunday dinner at big momma's house.

"Oh, you're about to find out real soon because I put my foot up in this food. But you can chill on the couch real quick while I put the finishing touches on my masterpiece." I handed Mo the remote and headed back to the kitchen.

I opened the oven to remove the foil from my ribs, and add a light glaze of barbeque sauce on top then let them bake for ten more minutes. My cornbread sat on top of the stove. It looked great as the top glistened with golden brown perfection. I could hear my greens lightly boiling as I turned the eye down to simmer. I was proud of my cooking, and I knew once Mo was done eating, he'd most likely want me for dessert. Good thing I grabbed a Pattie's sweet potato pie instead. I was trying to keep my cookies in the jar, so I needed something sweet to distract him. I loved Pattie's pie, so I had to pick one up. That young man wasn't playing when he sang about that pie, it is goodt with a t.

"10 more minutes, baby." I walked back over to the couch where Mo was sitting.

He looked up at me, and grabbed my hand to pull me down on the couch. "Okay, baby. Thank you again for inviting me into your lovely home, and cooking for me. You didn't have to do all this, so I really appreciate it." He kissed me on the cheek.

"Oh it was nothing, baby. I care about you, and I felt you deserved it." I looked him in his hazel eyes and kissed him. Butterflies filled my stomach as our lips touch.

For some reason, this kiss felt different from all the others. Over the past month, Mo and I were having an amazing time getting to know one another, and going on multiple dates during the week. I preferred being in public places because I don't allow everyone in my home; plus, I'm not a Netflix and chill type of chick. If you really want to get to know me, you will take the time and energy to court me. It wasn't about the money because I had that. It was about showing me that you weren't playing games with me. Mo had proven that, so my next step was having him over to my home. This was a big deal for me.

This was me showing him that my feelings for him were growing. As I kissed him, it felt so different because my heart was trying to tell me something. "Could this be love?" I thought to myself.

Beeeeeeppppp

I heard my timer from the oven go off. Thank goodness because I was all in my feelings kissing Mo.

"Sounds like dinner is ready. Would you like to sit at the table or keep chillin' on the couch?"

"Oh, I can eat on your fancy couch? You sure?" Mo looked at me with a look of uncertainty.

"Yea, silly, just don't drop nothing." I said, getting up from the couch and heading to the kitchen to fix our plates.

"Well, hell yea, I want to watch this game and get my grub on."

"Say no more, let me prepare your plate." I headed to the stove. "What do you want to drink?"

"Uuummm, you got a Sprite?"

"This is a no soda household, but I have sparkling water, regular water, and wine. Which would you prefer?"

"Just like a woman," he teased. "But I'll take a

sparkling water."

"Coming right up!"

I finished preparing his food, and took it to him along with his sparkling water.

"And dinner is served." I curtsied as I handed him his plate.

"Arianna, you didn't cook this! Where'd you order this from?" Mo looked at me with a serious face.

"Don't try me. Just because you get all this fineness don't mean I can't cook. Pretty girls can throw down too!" I snapped, with my hand on my hip and head cocked to the side.

"You tryna to make me propose cooking like this and looking like that! I found me a winner."

I giggled and walked back to the kitchen and fixed my plate. "Boy hush and eat your food."

Although I knew he was joking, deep down I wanted him to be serious. I wanted Mo to be the one. He's smart, he's successful, and he has a great sense of humor. Let's not forget how fine he is. What woman wouldn't want that? I just hoped we were growing at the same pace emotionally because I could really feel myself falling for him.

Mo and I ate our food together on the couch. Once we were done I gave him a slice of pie and we watched old episodes of Martin. I loved the feeling of just relaxing with him. It felt so good just being around him.

"Alright, let me wash these dishes."

"Aw nah, I can't let you do that. You worked too hard already, let me do it." Mo insisted.

"Aaawww, a man who washes dishes. You really know the way to my heart. How about I wash and you rinse?"

"Deal." Mo agreed, as he rolled up his sleeves and headed to the kitchen to help me.

I filled up the sink with water and soap and began washing. I handed Mo the first dish and he rinsed it and placed it in the dish rack to dry. We were almost done when I grabbed the pot that I cooked the collard greens in and dropped it in the water. I must've dropped it too hard because water splashed everywhere and went all over Mo.

I gasped. "I am so sorry, I did not mean to do that." I grabbed a dish towel and started dabbing his clothes.

"I don't believe you, you did that on purpose." Mo said, quickly dipping his hand in water and flicking it on me.

I screeched "Oh no you didn't! It's on now." I laughed as I grabbed the hose from the sink and started spraying Mo.

"Quit playing girl, quit playing!" Mo laughed and ran into the living room.

"Oh, don't run now!" I playfully chased him.

He then grabbed me, and pressed my body against his now wet sweater.

"Ahhh, noooo! Let me go!" I playfully wiggled, trying to get out of his grips.

"Nah girl, you did this to yourself!" He said, as he picked me up while falling backwards on the couch.

"Uh uh! Get off me, boy!" I laughed, suddenly looking deeply into his eyes.

Mo looked back at me, and we both felt the vibrations between us. He passionately kissed me. He wrapped his strong arms around my waist, and let his hand travel down every curve of my body. He reached my peach, and he squeezed it. The more his hands caressed my body, the more passionate our kiss became. Mo then lifted me up and flipped me over, so he was on top. He began to kiss me on my neck, I moaned. I let his tongue have its way with me as he traveled down to my double C breast. He pulled my shirt down revealing my areolas. He began to flick his tongue up and down on them. I felt an ocean begin to rise in my boy shorts. I was so ready for him, but he took his time. He put my left breast in his mouth, and began to suck with precision. He went from one breast to the other. I wrapped my legs around him and sank my nails in his back, letting him know I wanted more. He kissed my stomach and began to go down. He lightly glided his teeth over my pelvis area as he lifted my shirt and began to remove my tights with his tongue. I arched and lifted my back to help him get them off. Once removed, he continued to tease me with his tongue. He slid it from my pelvis to my inner thigh, flicking his tongue back and forth. I was so moist for him that I was leaking.

"Daddy I need it, give it to me." I purred as I begged for him to get inside of me.

"Not yet baby, let me get her wetter." He advised, as he sucked his index and middle and then put them inside of me.

I moaned louder. He stroked his fingers inside and out, while he continued to nibble on my inner thigh. I began moving my hips to the motion of his stroke. He placed his tongue on my clitoris, and began to do circles. He placed both of his hands around my thighs to grip me so I couldn't run. He increased the speed of the movement of his tongue.

"Daddy, you're about to make me cum." I mumbled, as I tried to wiggle away.

"Mmmm, hhhmmmm." He said, aggressively moving his tongue with the intention of making me reach my climax.

He circled his tongue a few more times, and I couldn't hold it any longer. I gasped and gripped his head for dear life. I felt my walls contract and passion filled my body. Mo stood up and removed his shirt revealing his six pack. I stood up before he could make another move and began to lick his entire chest, starting from his collar bone and worked my way down. Once I got to his belt, I removed it with my teeth as I looked up at him, square in the eyes. I unbuttoned his pants and took it out. I was very impressed with his nine-inch piece that had the perfect amount of girth. I dropped to my knees and went to work. I wrapped both hands around it and placed my mouth on the head.

I began to suck while my hands simultaneously twisted back and forth on the shaft. I increased my speed and intensity and Mo grabbed the back of my head; his grip got tighter and tighter. When I felt that he was about to cum, I stopped.

"No daddy, I need you inside of me."

I got up from my position, and bit his earlobe. He proceeded to lift me up by my thighs then moved me against the wall. He grabbed himself and entered me. I moaned and tightly wrapped my arms around his neck. He then began to slowly and deeply stroke. It felt so good that I was speechless. All I could do was moan and bite on his shoulder. I moved my face to meet his, and began sucking on his bottom lip. I moved my hips to match his intensity. The wetter I got, the faster we moved.

"Baby, I'm about to cum." Mo whispered, as his stroke became more aggressive.

"Come on daddy." I instructed as I pressed my body against his and held on tight as I bounced up and down on him, keeping the rhythm.

I felt his body jerk, and he began to slow down. He then looked me into my eyes and kissed me passionately, as he released himself. He dropped my legs slowly, trying to catch his breath. I then headed to the bathroom to clean myself up. I turned on the shower and got in. I heard Mo come into the bathroom.

"Are you going to join me baby?" I asked peeking around the shower curtain.

He looked at me and smiled, "Yea baby, I'm coming."

He entered the shower and we silently thought about what had just occurred as we washed one another. Once we got out, we went into my room and laid in the bed to cuddle. There was an awkward silence in the room. I couldn't believe I had given him the cookie after I said I wouldn't. Plus, I had broken single rule number six by not using a condom. I didn't know whether to feel excited because the sex was amazing, or ashamed because I felt that maybe we did it too soon and we didn't use protection. I just laid there, contemplating, not knowing what to say.

"So, are you on birth control?" Mo inquired nervously, breaking the silence.

"Negro, you picked a fine time to ask! But lucky for the both of us, yes I am. I just hope you're clean because we just did it like animals in there."

"I'm as clean as a whistle baby. You have nothing to worry about." Mo said as he wrapped his arms around me and pulled me closer to him.

He kissed me on my shoulder and I felt a little better. Maybe I was overthinking this. We had dated for a month and he didn't seem like the kind of guy to judge me off of how soon we had sex. It sucks being a woman because we constantly have to question if the man will leave after we give him the nookie. Some men will put on a great front and do everything right then once they get the cookie, they disappear. I prayed to myself Mo wouldn't do that. I had felt that pain before, and I didn't want to go through that again.

"Arianna, you know I'm not going anywhere, right?" Mo said as if he was reading my mind.

"Huh? Who said you were going anywhere?" I turned around to face him.

"No one, but I just wanted to reassure you that I'm here for you and I'm not going anywhere," he kissed me on the forehead.

I smiled and let out a sigh of relief "I'm really happy

to hear that." I kissed him on the lips and just looked into his eyes. They read that he was sincere and I believed him.

I felt I finally found someone who wouldn't leave me and would back up everything they said. My heart filled with hope and I watched Mo while he slept.

"I love you." I professed softly, before dozing off.

CHAPTER 6

What's Done in the Dark, Will Come to Light...

"So the real question is, did you get some cuddy that night?" Bianca asked in suspense.

"So, you wearing that pink dress I like right?"

"Mo, get off my phone! Bye!" I giggled while I dismissed Mo and his antics.

"Bye baby. See you tonight."

He told me he had a surprise for me tonight. I didn't know what it was, but I hope it consisted of him formally asking me to be his girlfriend. I know that sounds childish, but I assume nothing unless the man asks me specifically. Mo and I have been dating for three months now and I feel it's time. We spend almost every day together, plus I've been rocking his world in the bedroom ever since he came over for the first time. It's time he stepped up because I am not going to be anyone's single girlfriend. A single girlfriend is a chick who gives a man girlfriend benefits without actually being his girlfriend. It happens so much that most women forget they have no title. It doesn't come up until there's an argument about another woman and the guy hits her with "Well you aren't my girlfriend, so why are you mad?" Yep, I am not the one, and if he hits me with that I hope he's prepared to get hit with these hands. But I digress; I know I'm just overthinking. Mo is an amazing man. I would never have to worry about him playing me like that.

Bbzzzz bbbzzz bbbzzzz

I felt my phone buzz in my hand.

"Hey, Bianca, girl! Two weeks 'til the big day! AAAHHHH!!!" I shrieked in the phone. Bianca's wedding was only two weeks away, and I think I was just as excited as she was.

"OMG, I know! I can't believe I'm getting married. Oh my God, I'm getting married." Bianca began hyperventilating as she realized her current reality.

"Bish, if you don't calm your dramatic ass down." I stared blankly at the phone in my hand. I was completely over Bianca's Bridezilla routine. She had been acting like a nutcase for the past two months. I knew planning a wedding was hard, but she was taking it way too far.

"But no, Arianna, this is real. Like, it's actually about to happen. What if something goes wrong? What if my dress gets stained? What if my white peacocks get lost on the way to the venue?"

"Girl, if you don't stop! You are about to marry a fine ass, successful black man, with no kids! And this nigga agreed to give you white peacocks at the wedding! If I was in front of you, I'd pluck you right in the forehead. Smack dab in the middle. Hard, too!" I chastised B, trying to get her to recognize that she was doing way too much and needed to be happy versus dramatic in this moment.

Bianca calmed her breathing, "You're right, you're right. Getting a man like that, with no kids, is something like a blessing. Especially getting him before Becky with the good hair snatches him up. When he proposed, I felt like Oprah in The Color Purple. All my life I had to fight!" We both started cracking up at Bianca mimicking the famous line from The Color Purple.

"Seriously though, don't stress yourself out. Your day is gonna be perfect. I'll fight a bish before I let anyone ruin it. That's what the Maid of Honor is here for. I'm supposed to be stressed, not you." I assured B that her wedding would be perfect. "But most importantly, I'm here to make this bachelorette party litty! Ayyyyeeeee." I began to Milly Rock as if B could see me.

"Arianna, I told you I want a chill bachelorette party." B pleaded.

"No chill, got it." I contradicted B's previous statement.

"Arianna, I'm not kidding. I don't want anything cr—"

"Oh no, I'm late for my doctor's appointment. Byeeee." I rushed Bianca off the phone before she could finish her sentence. I refused to let her convince me that she wanted a chill bachelorette party. She knew I was incapable of doing any such thing. How dare she try to make me water down anything that pertained to a party? The nerve of her.

I placed my phone on the kitchen counter and walked into my room to grab my jacket so I could head to my doctor's appointment. I was going to my gynecologist for my annual checkup. During the exam, I got tested for every single STD there was. I had to make sure I was good because STDs don't discriminate. Neither does pregnancy. Mo and I hadn't been using protection, but I was on birth control so I wasn't worried. I really trust him, and even if I was pregnant, I wouldn't be worried. I'm not ready for kids, but if I were to have a baby by Mo I wouldn't be devastated.

"Little Mo Jr. or Moesha. I like the sound of that." I pondered as I daydreamed of what a life with Mo would be like if we were married with kids.

"Okay, these mystery rides are getting old." I complained to Mo as we drove to wherever he was taking me. He had picked me up thirty minutes ago and had yet to tell me where we were going.

"Girl hush, you know you love my surprises." Mo teased, as he looked at me grinning with his dimples showing.

He was right, I loved his surprises. "Shut up" Looking away so he couldn't see my crimson cheeks. He still gave me butterflies just like the first day we met at the mailbox.

"We're almost there though, so calm down."

Mo reassured.

Bzzz bbzzz bbzzz

Mo's phone rang.

"Aren't you gonna get that. That's the third time, somebody blowing you up."

Mo picked up the phone from the cup holder and looked to see who was calling. He then took a deep breath and rolled his eyes before placing the phone face down, back in the cup holder.

"Damn, who pissed in your Cheerios?" I looked at Mo concerned.

"It's this client. He wants me to go in with him on this new startup app, but I'm still deciding." Mo took his left hand and wiped his face. He seemed very flustered.

"Well, what's the name of the app?" I adjusted my body towards him. I wanted to hear more so maybe I could help him make the decision.

"Uuuhhh…I think it's…something with a S. I don't know, but I don't want to talk about that right now. Tonight is about us." Mo brushed it off.

"You sure? I mean I can help you de—"

"I'm positive baby, I got it." Mo said, cutting me off

before I could finish my statement.

"Alright, sir." I threw my hands up and turned my body back around. It wasn't like Mo to cut me off, or not want to fully discuss matters. This client must've really pissed him off. I didn't want to ruin our night, so I left it alone. The car filled with awkward silence for the rest of the ride.

"Lil' Rel and friends…" I said, reading a black billboard with white writing in the distance. I loved Lil' Rel ever since he was the hero in the hit movie *Get Out*. I had been wanting to see him live, but every time he came into town I was too busy.

"Baby, did you know Lil' Rel was in town? I hate that I always miss his shows." I turned to look at Mo, trying to loosen up the tension in the car.

"Lil' Rel, who dat?"

"T, S, mothafuckin' A! You know, the guy with the Netflix special I forced you to watch, and you were crying laughing the entire time."

Mo reached in the cup holder and grabbed his phone. He fumbled with it a little while trying to make sure he kept his eyes on the road. He then handed me his phone. "Oh, you mean this Lil' Rel right here?"

I grabbed the phone and began smiling from ear to ear. I started jumping up and down in my seat like a kid headed to Disney World. "OMG, OMG, OMG!!!! You got us tickets!" I unwrapped the top part of the seatbelt and leaned over and started kissing Mo repeatedly on his lips and cheeks.

"Daddy, knows what you like." Mo smirked arrogantly.

"Oh, so you daddy now?" I shot a sharp look over to Mo. "When did you become that?"

"When you called me that last night when I had your legs pinned to the headboard. Daddy, oh daddy, please!" Mo mimicked in the best female voice he could conjure up.

I start playfully hitting him while I laughed the embarrassment away, "You get on my nerves!" I sat back in my seat and folded my arms with my lip poked out.

Mo pulled into the parking lot. There was a long line of cars waiting to be valeted. He looked over at me pouting and leaned over to kiss me, but I blocked him. "Don't be like that baby," he said, laughing. "I'm just playing with you. You my lil' momma." He said, as he grabbed my chin, turning my face towards him to kiss me repeatedly on the lips. He always knew how to cheer me up. I could never stay mad at him for long. I may as well wear a t-shirt that read "I'm sprung" because that's exactly what I was.

The valet lightly tapped our window to get our attention. If he would have come two minutes later, he would've gotten a freak show for free because there was no telling how far we would've gone in that car.

Once we got into the building, we waited for the hostess to seat us. It was a packed house. Since Lil' Rel was a part of Kevin Hart's team, I believe everyone was there to see if Kevin Hart would show up. I would love to see them both. After waiting for ten minutes, the hostess escorted us to the front row. Once at our table, I looked at Mo with discomfort.

"Why in the hell would you get seats right in the front? He's going to light our asses up with these jokes." I grumbled, as I stood there looking around for someone we could trade tables with.

Mo began to chuckle "Relax, we'll be fine. We just have to laugh at all the jokes so he knows we're on his side."

I rolled my eyes still not convinced. "I guess." I sat my purse and jacket down on the table. "I'm going to run to the restroom to make sure I look my best for my roast session." I said sarcastically, as I walked away leaving Mo at the table shaking his head at my dramatics.

As I made my way to the restroom, I felt like a gazelle in a lion's den. So many men stalked me with their eyes that it was just downright disrespectful. I couldn't lie; I knew I was looking like a snack. I wore the dress Mo loved so much. It was a blush colored mini dress with a slight split on the left thigh. It was spaghetti strapped and fit my curves perfectly. I paired it with a chunky rose gold choker with rose gold, open toe, strappy heels to match. My hair was bone straight with a middle part, and I had Brazilian inches for days that stopped right above my Georgia peach. I knew I looked edible, but most of these dudes were with their lady. I wish Mo would be staring at another chick like these guys were staring at me. He'd catch this fade, too quick.

"Arianna! Arianna! Hold up!" I heard a familiar male voice yell behind me. It didn't sound like Mo, but I knew it was familiar. I thought maybe I heard wrong so I just kept walking.

"Arianna! Please, wait up!" Okay, that time, I know I heard it. I quickly stopped and turned around, searching for the person the voice belonged to. When I finally saw the familiar face, my heart dropped into my stomach. It was like that feeling you get when you reach the top of a rollercoaster, and the rollercoaster goes straight down, and you feel as if your heart is in your stomach. My forehead began to sweat, and my heart began to beat so hard that I thought it was going to jump out of my chest. I was in so much shock that I just stood there, staring, not knowing what to do. My brain said run into the bathroom, but my feet didn't move. I was stuck there in shock.

"Arianna, I don't even know what to say. I can't believe you're here. It's so good to see you. You look breathtaking." There he was; Keith stood there, right in front of me. He tried to lean in for a hug, but my body finally began doing what my brain told it to, and I put one hand up to stop him.

"What you want, Keith?" I said, taking a deep breath and dropping my shoulders to show my frustrations.

"I just wanna talk. Can we step over to the lobby area real quick?" Keith looked desperate. I hadn't seen him in over six months. He had been reaching out to me, but I ignored every contact attempt. "Please, just five minutes," he begged.

I contemplated for a second because I really didn't feel like hashing this out right now, but he looked desperate. I had never seen him like this, and I felt bad. I rolled my eyes and responded "Okay, five minutes. But that's all you get because I'm on a date and this is disrespectful to him."

"Okay, no problem, five minutes I promise." Keith said, relieved as we headed to the foyer to get some privacy.

When we got there, Keith just stared at me. I stared back with my face curled up giving him all the attitude I could muster up, annoyed by why he wanted to talk so badly. "Umm…hello. You're wasting your five minutes, now you got four. Speak."

"Oh..uh..I'm sorry. I haven't seen you in so long I'm just really nervous, and you're so beautiful I just don't… I mean, I can't find the words to say." Keith fumbled over his words. I was honestly shocked because he was a man of many words and usually well spoken. Maybe he was genuinely sorry. At this point, I didn't care much because he had taken the biggest dump on my heart; so why should I care about his.

I waved my hand in the air dismissing his compliment

"Boy, I ain't tryna hear all that. Three minutes." I stood there with my hands on my hips waiting for him to say something of substance.

"I'm sorry, alright. I'm really sorry, Arianna. If I could take it all back I would but I'm manning up right now and telling you I'm sorry." Keith just stood there, waiting anxiously for my response.

"You're sorry, huh? What are you sorry for? Telling me that you wouldn't hurt me, but then disappearing with no explanation? Oh, or blocking me from social media and your phone so I had no way to contact you? Oh, or are you sorry for telling me you loved me and wanted a future with me just so I could see you on Facebook with another chick two weeks after you disappeared? Oh, you thought I didn't know, huh? Yea, everything in the dark must come to light. You needed time my ass; you had a whole 'nother bitch, but you love me, huh? Fuck you, Keith." I felt warmth press my cheek as tears began to fall. I couldn't believe I was wasting another tear on this fool. I was so done with this conversation. There was nothing else to say or hear. He wasn't even willing to fess up. I turned around to walk away, I was over it.

"Arianna, wait! Please! I love you, I'm in love with you. Don't leave me, I need you." Keith's voice trembled as he pleaded with me not to walk away.

I stopped and turned around to look at Keith, face full of tears. "Keith, I can't do this right now." I then turned and started speed walking to the bathroom, leaving Keith standing there.

I was a wreck. I didn't know what to do. I didn't want Mo to see me like this. I also didn't need to completely ruin my makeup either because that would make my roast session worse, seeing that we were on the first row. I made it to the bathroom to see my lashes and liner were still intact. That NYX finishing spray was no joke. All I need to do was blend my makeup on the parts that were tear stained. I took a paper towel and started dabbing my cheeks. After two minutes of dabbing, I felt my face was as good as new. My eyes were still super puffy though, so I wanted to wait before walking back to my table. I was so out of it that I didn't catch the side eye of this chick staring at me out of the corner of my eye. I was not in the mood and I was ready for somebody to pop off. I turned my head to the left prepared for whatever she was about to say.

"So, is there a problem?" I turned, looking directly at the mystery girl staring at me.

"Huh? Who, me?" The girl asked, baffled that I was speaking to her so harshly.

"Yea, you. You've been staring a hole in my damn face, so I'm tryna see if there's a problem."

"Oh no, girl! I'm sorry. I was staring at you because you look mad familiar. I think we used to work together. Weren't you a waitress at Brews?"

"Yea, I did, way back in like '09. Girl, that's a memory I wish to forget." We both laughed.

"I knew I remembered you. You quit that one day and spazzed out on everybody. It took Bianca to calm you down cuz you were on 1,000." she stated with confidence, as she fully remembered a time I fully wanted to forget.

I shook my head and covered my face with embarrassment. "Girl, please don't remind me of a much more ghetto time."

We both laughed. "So, how's B? I haven't seen her in forever?"

"She's great! She gets married in two weeks, and

I'm throwing her bachelorette party next weekend. You should come! I know she would love to see you."

Her face lit up with excitement. "Yes! I would love to! Take my number." She reached her hand out for my phone, and I handed it to her.

"And what's your name again, girl. I am horrible with names."

"You good, I am too. I'm Kendra. I only remember your name because you're the most talked about employee that ever worked at Brews." She handed my phone back to me.

"Now if I invite you to this party, you can't bring this up again. I keep my ratchicity under wraps these days, so I can't have those boujee broads know that side of me." We both made our way out of the bathroom.

Kendra smiled, "Your secret is safe with me." We hugged one another before we parted ways. "Enjoy the show!" Kendra said, as she walked away. I was glad I saw her. It gave me a chance to calm down and regroup after that Keith nonsense. Now I was ready to get my laugh on, and prepare for my possible roast session.

As I approached the table, I saw Mo on a heated phone conversation. I felt like it was the client from the car, but he was acting strange so I slowly crept up so I could eavesdrop on the conversation.

"I'm going to be there next week, damn! Stop pressuring me. I just found out about this damn baby, what do you expect me to do?" Mo said, shouting into the phone at whomever he was speaking to.

"Baby? Who the fuck has a baby?" I thought to myself. I continued to slowly approach the table.

"I'm out with a client, I gotta go. Bye." Mo quickly ended the call and slammed his phone on the table. He dropped his head in his hand, he look really frustrated.

"A meeting with a client? Why did he lie?" I started to add things together in my head about how awkward Mo acted in the car, and how he was having this heated phone conversation with this strange person. My gut told me there was something very fishy going on and I may need to unveil my rachicity, but I was too weak emotionally and I didn't know the full details.

"Hey baby, sorry it took so long. I ran into an old friend from work and we got to chatting, and I totally lost track of time. Did I miss anything?" I approached the table as if I didn't just hear what happened on the phone. I didn't want to start anything, and I wanted more time to gather evidence. I also wanted to see if Mo would tell me the truth about whatever he had going on.

Mo looked up startled "Oh nah, baby, the show hasn't even started. Don't ever leave me that long though, you know I start missing you and break out into hives." Mo said trying to play off how frustrated he was.

I gave a slight grin, trying to hide the fact that I knew he was lying. I took my seat and decided that whatever he had going on would be tomorrow's issue. I wanted to enjoy the night, and forget about the Keith drama. I'd get my inspector gadget on tomorrow about Mo.

"Waiter, can I please have a bottle of Patron with salt and limes." I requested, flagging the waiter down.

"Damn baby, you aight?" Mo asked worried.

"Oh, I'm just peachy." I lied. "Unless there's something I should be upset about?"

"What? Nah baby, you trippin'. Don't start acting crazy now."

"I'm going to show you crazy, you just wait." I mumbled, as I thought about the events of the evening. So much for getting that girlfriend proposal tonight. I keep telling Bianca I'm cursed, she's going to listen to me one day.

CHAPTER 7

Bachelorette Pity Party

"Got yo ass, now! In this picture, holding this baby. Who you thought you we—oh wait, that's his nephew." I said to myself, as I snooped through all of Mo's Instagram photos for the fifth time.

Ever since that night at the comedy club, I spent about thirty minutes every day on my investigation. Call me crazy if you want, but I get the answers I need in order to build a case against anyone. I low key missed my calling as a detective. I had been searching for an entire week for any signs that Mo may have a baby or baby momma and I hadn't found anything but several nieces, nephews, and cousins. I went through each picture searching through comments from other women and clicking on their profiles to research. Most those heffas' pages were private and I couldn't request them because that's just crazy. But from a week of my level ten Inspector Gadget mode, I hadn't found anything. I didn't know if I was happy or not that I didn't find anything. A part of me wanted to find something because it would explain the drama that occurred last Saturday in the car, and when I heard Mo on the phone. The other part of me wanted to believe that Mo wasn't hiding anything, and maybe that was just his sister on the line.

"But that wouldn't explain why he lied and said he was out with a client. AAAHHHH!" I roared in frustration and chugged my glass of wine until it was gone.

My intuition told me there was something up, so I knew I just had to figure it out. There have been so many times where my intuition told me something was off and I hoped and wished I was wrong, but I was always right. Men never understand a woman's intuition, but it is so real. I pray this is the first time I'm wrong, and that Mo will just tell me without me having to ask.

"Message" my phone sang alerting me that I had received a text.

> Hi Arianna, I just wanted to confirm the three male strippers you booked for the evening. They will arrive at your Westin suite at 8PM this evening.

"Yyyaaasssss!" I cheered getting up from my barstool excited about the evening. It was finally the day of Bianca's bachelorette party and it was about to be a night she would never forget.

I had requested three male strippers for the evening. One piece of dark chocolate, one piece of light chocolate, and one midget stripper just to warm the crowd up. I even had 4 male models booked that would serve the ladies shirtless for the entire evening. I booked The Cooking Bachelor as the caterer, so I knew the food would be impeccable. This was an all men everything type of party. I know B wanted it to be chill, but I refused to allow her to stop my shine. She knew not what she needed.

I picked up my phone and dialed Bianca's older sister's number. She was eight years older than B and they were extremely close. Vicki was surprising B from Houston. She had flown in yesterday to help me set up the room, and she was actually going to pick B up using my car and bring her to the party. I couldn't wait to see B's face.

"Hey, Vicki, girl! You ready for the big night?" I bubbled with excitement.

"Yas, hunty! I can't believe I was able to hold this secret from Bianca for so long. You know she's nosey and done asked me 50 million questions. I'm glad I can let the cat out the bag tonight."

"I applaud you too! Lord knows it was hard for me to keep it from her because she's tricky. She knows how to ask the right questions and get you all the way caught up. That sneaky little heffa." We both laughed.

"So, you're meeting me at the Westin at 5PM, right, so I can get your car and go get her?"

"Yes ma'am, be ready. I need you to turn off all your inhibitions because we're getting litty tonight!!!"

"You so crazy," Vicki giggled "See you soon boo!"

She said before ending the call.

"Let me call Mo real quick before I get too busy with the party." I scrolled through my call log looking for his number. I hadn't heard from him all day which wasn't like him. I dialed the number and let the phone ring until the voicemail.

"Hmm, that's strange." I thought to myself while staring at the phone, wondering why I hadn't heard from Mo all day. I decided to send him a text.

> Hey baby, just thinking about you. Hit me back when you get a chance.

Now that I think about it, we hadn't talked much at all this week. I was too busy being Nancy Drew to realize our distance. We had only been talking through text and they were really short. This had me really starting to worry. I am a firm believer that when the conversation is getting shorter with you, it's getting longer with someone else. I tried to push the thought of Mo doing dirt in the back of my head so I could focus on my Maid of Honor duties. I needed to be dressed and ready for set up in two hours. Mo drama would just have to wait until after the party.

* * *

"I need the penis cupcakes over there by the pole. Yes, right next to the penis straws." I directed the room service attendee as we set up for the bachelorette party of the century.

I had rented out the penthouse luxury suite at the Westin hotel, and it was worth every penny. The room was customized for the bride to be, and equipped with a stripper pole, a bar, and an incredible view of the city. The room had two levels and plenty of space for the ladies who weren't going to make it home. I had a strict no drinking and driving policy, and I even bought pajamas for the ladies who would have to stay the night. Bianca wasn't big on drinking, but I knew the best parties had to be stocked with the best liquor. I had every flavor of Ciroc from vanilla to pineapple, Hennessey because Hennything is possible, and five bottles of Ace of Spades because we start with straight shots and then pop bottles. I had turkey burger sliders, lemon pepper wings, fried chicken, fried tilapia, a veggie and fruit platter, and plenty of French fries because that was Bianca's favorite. I needed hardy food because I didn't want hangovers. I also had penis cupcakes, penis straws, and penis shaped cups. I may have overdone it with the penis welcome mat, but you only live once. I had everything set up and I was just waiting on the ladies to arrive so I could text Vicki and tell her the coast was clear to bring B.

"Message!" my text message alert sounded off.

Hey girl, I'm downstairs, what's the room number.

I rolled my eyes in disappointment because I was hoping it was from Mo. I had called and texted him four hours ago, and I hadn't heard back from him. Don't you hate when you're waiting on a certain someone to respond, and you get pissed at everyone else for texting and calling you because it isn't who you want it to be? That's exactly how I felt. I was starting to think something was wrong because Mo had never done this before. I didn't want to stalk him by messaging and calling again, but I was really getting worried. I guess one more text won't hurt.

> Baby, are you okay? I'm starting to get worried.

I sent the text to Mo praying that he was okay, and that I would hear from him soon. I then responded to the first guest letting her know the room number. I took a deep breath to calm myself down. I couldn't let Mo throw me off my game. I was the Maid of Honor, so I had to pull my shit together. Couldn't let anyone see me sweat. Today was about B, and that's all that mattered.

Once the first guest arrived, it set off a chain reaction because my phone went off every five minutes after that. I didn't realize how many ladies we had invited. I know fifty ladies RSVP'd, but sheesh, I didn't think they'd all actually show up. I was happy I splurged and got the biggest suite or else there wouldn't have been enough room.

"Hey boo, can you make sure each lady gets a cup?" I handed one of the shirtless models a tray full of the

Bianca cocktail that was really just a Sex on the Beach with a splash of champagne.

The ladies whistled and made sexual remarks at the model as he handed them their drinks. I even saw one of the ladies grab is man parts.

"Chill, girl! You tryna go to jail for sexual harassment? They don't discriminate. Sheesh!" I said to the horny sister that was damn near trying to rape the guy as he walked by her. Women were worse than men sometimes. I can tell these freaks hadn't had any in a while, I felt sorry for the strippers already.

We're in the lobby, you ready?

I received the text from Vicki confirming that the coast was clear for her to bring B up. I let her know we were ready, and began to prepare the ladies for her entry.

"Okay, ladies! B is coming up right now! Let's turn up one time for the bride to be!" I enthused, pumping the ladies up for B's entrance. All the ladies started getting hype and I knew this would be an unforgettable night.

I heard the knock at the door letting me know it was

time for B to come in. I looked down and hit play on my phone.

"She's your, queen to beeeee…" The speakers rang out the wedding song from the movie *Coming to America*.

I motioned for two of the male models to get in position. The room was dimly lit, and Vicki led B to a throne like chair while the song played in the background. All the ladies hid as Bianca sat down on her throne. Two male models approached the chair and lifted it while she remained seated. I could hear her pleading with them not to drop her as they carried the chair to the center of the room. As soon as the shirtless models sat her down, I hit next on my Apple Music app, and Beyoncé's Single Ladies began playing. The lights flicked on, and everyone jumped out from their hiding places.

"SURPISE!!!!" Everyone yelled, running up to the bride to be.

Tears instantly stained Bianca's face as she took in what had just happened. "Oh my God, Arianna, I said small." Bianca giggled through her tears.

"Yea, I know you said that, but I knew your heart wanted big because if not, you wouldn't have put me in charge." I wiped the tears from Bianca's face. "Now, turn up one time! You getting married!" I started to Milly Rock and everyone joined in.

"Ayyeee, ayyyeee, ayyyeee," everyone chanted while they did their best Single Ladies dance with Bianca.

I stood back and took a look at my hard work. I had been planning this party for three months, and I was so happy that it all came together. B deserved the best of everything. She had been through a lot with men, just as much as me, but she took the disciplined route and became celibate while she waited for her husband. I admired how she was able to do that, and be completely alone and content. I thought she was a robot sometimes. Well her formula worked, I just didn't know if I could do that.

"Could you be celibate while you wait for your soulmate?" I contemplated the thought of withholding sex until marriage. I burst out laughing "Girl please, you can't go two minutes without thinking about sex, how you gone be celibate?" I shook my head knowing I was kidding myself with even thinking about celibacy. That was damn near impossible for me.

"Hey girl, I think the surprise is here." Vicki informed me discreetly.

"Yaassss! Let me go get them, and you get the ladies ready."

I walked out into the hallway to see three men standing in trench coats. One guy was chocolate with a full beard that connected to his side burns. He gave you that Kofi Siriboe look, but he had muscles everywhere; I could see them through the coat. Next to him was a caramel snack with some Spanish flavor. He had a cute curly afro that was brown with blonde streaks, green eyes with thick brown eyebrows, and his face was freshly shaved to show off his high cheek bones. He was every bit of my type. Lastly, it was my favorite, the fun sized snack. I looked down to see the midget stripper. He was about four feet tall, and light skinned with a fade. He grinned as I looked at him to show off his perfect teeth and his dimples. He was a little cutie, and I could tell he was fit too. If I didn't prefer my men tall, I might've given him a shot.

"I like, I like. I hope y'all can dance as good as y'all look." I approved, looking each of them in the eye.

"Oh baby, we got that. I just hope you tip as good as

you look." The fun sized snack said to me, as he looked me up and down.

"Uh, okay then! We got a cocky one." I laughed. "Well let me sneak y'all in real quick, we're going to speed walk to the left when I open the door." I gently cracked the door, peeking my head in to make sure the coast was clear for the strippers to come in.

Once I saw that everyone was preoccupied dancing, I motioned for the guys to come in. Once they were in the back room, I ran down the order each of them would be going in. They all nodded their heads, and I asked them which songs they'd prefer. They gave me the list, and I nodded to let them know I understood. I then exited the room and headed to get the ladies ready for the climax of the night.

"Alright ladies, can I have your attention please!" I shouted over the music, "So you know those cupcakes ain't the only snacks I brought tonight. And you know I like to bring a variety of snacks cuz I know some people like different thangs. So, raise your hands if you like chocolate snacks, ladies?"

I waited and let the ladies raise their hands.

"Well, what about a little caramel in your life?" I probed, as I walked back in forth increasing anticipation.

"Okay ladies, I see y'all feeling the delectable treats I brought. But I bet y'all didn't know there's another type of snack, and it ain't vanilla."

"But I like cream in my coffee." One of the ladies said as she poked her lip out. Everyone burst out laughing.

"I feel you girl, but I got something better than that. You know what I got?" I asked rhetorically, flowing into a dramatic pause waiting for the ladies to be at their highest peak of anticipation.

"A ffffuuuunnnnn sssnnnaaaaccckkkkk!!!!" I pressed play, queuing the first stripper to come out. *Tootsie Roll* played loudly in the speaker.

My fun sized snack came out the back, and all the ladies went crazy. He walked out with his trench coat slightly open and his shoulders back like he was ready to put on the best show. As soon as he was right in the middle of the crowd, he ripped his jacket off and began to gyrate his entire body.

"Damn!" I said to myself, admiring his physique.

This little man had muscles everywhere. I don't think

he had an inch of body fat. That definitely got rid of the myth in my head that midgets couldn't be fit. That's a damn lie. Once he was done gyrating his body, he then flipped over into a handstand and started popping. Ones began to fly everywhere; the ladies were feeling my fun sized snack. I cocked my head to the side because I was highly impressed. How did he learn to do these things?

Knock knock knock

I looked down at my watch and it was 10:45PM. I wondered who it could be this late. I hope no one had complained about noise because they were going to have to get over it. We were just getting started. I walked over to the door, annoyed that someone was making me miss the show. I looked through the peephole and saw Kendra.

I quickly opened the door "Hey, girl! I thought you weren't going to make it." I hugged her as she walked through the door.

"I wouldn't miss this girl! But sorry I'm so late, my sister's baby shower ran over, then she was in her emotions and I had to help her clean up after the party. Girl, it was just a big 'ol mess." Kendra explained, after walking through the door and taking her jacket off.

"You good girl, they're too lit to pay attention anyway. I got a snack performing right now." I laughed and pointed to fun sized, who was now licking whipped cream off of one of the ladies.

"Where can I put my stuff?" Kendra inquired, holding her purse, jacket, and a paper bag with what looked to be a bottle of alcohol in it.

"In there." I pointed towards a table that held guest items.

"Thanks, girl. Oh, and here." She went to give me the paper bag she held in her hand, and mistakenly dropped her phone.

I stooped down to pick up her phone, but when I flipped it over the picture I saw caught me in my throat. I held the phone in my hand, and slowly picked it up from the floor. I thought I was dreaming; I couldn't believe what I was seeing. There it was; a picture of a baby shower. A beautiful light skinned woman with curly hair stood there looking like she was ready to pop with a sign above her head that read "It's a Girl". I followed her hand as it was connected to a man I knew. A man I had trusted and given my heart to. There Mo was, standing next to a woman who was ready to give birth. I stood there stuck with my mouth slightly open, not really knowing what to do.

"Oh, that's my sister and her child's father. They were together, but I don't really know what they're doing now. He's so flip flop, but whatever. That's Mo for you." Kendra said, explaining the picture I looked at.

I was speechless, I couldn't say anything. I just stood there, still gazing at the picture. I heard someone saying my name but it sounded so distant because I wasn't in this world anymore. I was totally zoned out.

"Arianna," Kendra shook me, "Are you okay? You need water or anything?"

I finally snapped out of my trance and handed her the phone back. I shook my head to get myself back together. "Oh yea," I responded softly, "I'm fine, go join the party. I'm gonna run to the restroom really quick." I used all of my strength to hold back the tears forming in my eyes.

"You sure?" Kendra said with uncertainty, looking as if she didn't want to leave my side.

"Yea girl, I'll be fine. I just got a little hot flash, I guess. Probably from all this running around I've been doing for the party." I lied. "But no, go and join the party, I'll be right out. The next guy is coming up soon and you don't want to miss him, I promise." I faked a slight smile so Kendra would believe me.

She finally walked away and I headed to the bathroom. As soon as the door closed, I instantly started bawling. I leaned my back against the wall and slid down. All I could do was cry. I couldn't believe this was happening to me again. I felt like I had just gotten hit by a car. Physically, my entire body hurt. I felt so many emotions. I was angry, hurt, sad, confused, and just broken. It felt like déjà vu. I had just gone through this exact thing six months ago with Keith, now Mo. What did I do to deserve this? I was a good person and I never intentionally harmed anyone. Why was God punishing me? I didn't get it. I didn't deserve it.

Bang Bang Bang

I heard hard knocks at the door.

"Arianna, we need the music for the second stripper. The first is done." yelled Vicki through the door.

I mustered up my energy to respond. "Okay girl, I'll be right out." I pulled myself off the floor and looked in the mirror.

My eyes were bloodshot red and puffy. I knew I couldn't hide in the bathroom all night, so I splashed water on my face in attempts to pull myself together.

"This night is about B. This isn't about me."

I couldn't let this drama ruin Bianca's night, I had to finish what I started. I took a deep breath, then turned around to walk out the door to see Vicki standing there waiting.

"Omg, girl, are you okay? It looks like you've been crying." Vicki asked sympathetically.

"Oh no, girl, I'm fine. My allergies are horrible. My eyes get puffy and I get the sniffles. I'll be alright though. The show must go on."

"Oh I totally understand. My husband is the exact same way."

We both walked back towards the living room area where all the other ladies were. I must've done a great job lying because she believed me. Once I got to the living room, I played the next song and the chocolate drop came out. All the ladies were mesmerized, but I had heartbreak on my mind. I decided that if I had to finish the night out, I may as well numb myself. I walked to the bar and grabbed a bottle of Ace of Spades. I popped the cork and toasted it up to the air.

"Yolo!" I declared before tipping the entire bottle up and chugging all of it. I just wanted to numb the pain.

CHAPTER 8

Baby Daddy of the Year

I parted my eyelids in an attempt to fully wake myself up.

"Aaahhhh" I groaned in agony. My head was pounding. I really shouldn't have drunk two bottles of champagne last night.

I heard knocks from the front door of the hotel. I assumed it was room service. "Go away." I said faintly remembering that I had forgotten to put the "Do not Disturb" sign on the door.

I had been at the hotel since Saturday night and it was now Monday morning. I was too weak to pack everything and clean up so I just paid for another night at the room. I also didn't feel like going back home to face my reality. I felt like I was in the middle of a soap opera. I really couldn't believe my life was real. The man I had fallen in love with in such a short time had betrayed me. I just knew I was going to wake up and this would all be a dream, but it wasn't. Mo really had a whole baby on the way with some beautiful woman, who just so happened to be my home girl's sister.

I peeled myself off the couch in an attempt to grab my phone from the charger. As I picked myself up to walk, I could feel my legs about to give out.

"One foot in front of the other, you got this Arianna." I coached myself as I attempted to walk across the room.

Boom! "Ow!" I said grabbing my foot after hitting it on the coffee table. "Dammit! What did I do to deserve this?!" I yelled to the ceiling.

I'm convinced that God really doesn't like me. He really knew how to kick a sista while she was down. I made my way over to the bar where my phone was. I picked it up to check to see if anyone had called. I had several texts from the ladies from Saturday night just thanking me for a good time. I hadn't let anyone know what was going on because I didn't want to ruin the evening. I'd rather sulk in solitude than have everyone throw a pity party for me when it was supposed to be Bianca's day. As I scrolled up, I had four missed calls from Mo and six unread text messages. My eyes filled with tears looking at his name in my notifications. I dropped my head and began crying again.

I know I hadn't known Mo for that long, but I trusted him. We had been dating for a little over three months, and I really did see a future with him. We had talked about marriage, babies, and traveling the world together. I had never seen any signs that he had another woman pregnant the entire time we were dating. I honestly didn't know how to handle the situation. I wanted to just ignore him because he had a family now, and I didn't want to interfere with that. But the other part of me felt that he owed me an explanation for everything. Maybe if I got answers I could move on from the situation. I really didn't know what to do, but I knew I wasn't ready to speak to him at that moment. I guess I'd get myself together and prepare to head home. Maybe then I could read his text messages and decide what to do next. In the meantime, I'll take a shot of this Ciroc to help my headache. It's happy hour somewhere.

After my shot, I decided to clean up and prepare to head home. I packed everything from the hotel that I felt I could use. I left the rest in the room in trash bags so the housekeepers could remove them. I really could've just left the room a mess seeing that cleaning is a part of what I paid for that expensive ass room. But I could hear my momma's voice in my head "If you keep a dirty house, then folks will think you keep dirty drawers, too." I rolled my eyes at the thought because she was really reaching. Like who really thought that way? Honestly, I didn't give a damn what anybody thought right now. I was leaving with a broken heart I hadn't come with. I felt crappy, and looked it as well. I hadn't combed my hair or wiped off my makeup from Saturday night. I wore huge gray sweatpants with Nike flip-flops, and a blue Nike jacket. I wore shades to cover the puffiness of my eyes because I hadn't stopped crying since the incident happened. I took the last bit of strength I had and brushed my teeth because stank breath is downright disrespectful. I probably looked homeless, but I could care less. I just wanted to stop by the store, grab several bottles of wine, and go home and mend my broken heart in peace.

I pulled up to the QT by my house and parked my car by the pump. There were always so many people at QT, no matter what time of the day. It always looked like a club or something. I saw a group of guys standing outside by the door, and I prayed they wouldn't stop me seeing that I looked like an entire bum. I took a deep breath to try to recoup some type of energy, then I took my key out of the ignition and got out of the car. Once my foot hit the concrete, I began speed walking towards the door with my resting bitch face in full effect. I went straight to the wine and grabbed four bottles of sweet, red wine. I would've grabbed more, but that was all I could carry in my arms without fear that they'd fall.

"Hi ma'am, how are you?" The clerk asked, as I approached the register.

"Oh, I'm fucking horrible. I just found out the man I

love has a whole baby on the way, and I had no fucking idea. And you?" I thought to myself.

But I knew I couldn't say that without the clerk being frightened for their life and maybe wanting to call security. When most people asked how you were, they didn't want the truth. So I gave the politically correct response by putting on a slight smile and giving the clerk a thumb up.

"That'll be $26.65." The clerk stated as she began to bag my wine.

I swiped my card and waited for the approval. I then grabbed my bags and prepared to walk away. I thanked the clerk then exited the store, beginning my power walk and readjusting my face to resting bitch mode. As soon as I hit the door, I saw one the guys in the group run up to grab it.

"Oh wait lil' momma, let me get that for you." A guy with sagging skinny jeans said, running to open the door for me.

I never understood that. The jeans were made skinny to fit, right? Why in the hell would you sag them? I gave a slight smile, then went right back to bitch face and speed walk.

"Can I talk to you real quick?" asked Mr. Skinny Sag, as he slightly jogged to catch up to me.

I rolled my eyes underneath my shades. Why didn't men read body language? My entire demeanor read, "Leave me the hell alone," but here he was chasing me.

"So, what's your name?"

"I don't have one." I grumbled.

He laughed, "You funny. But forreal though, I'd like to get to know you."

"No, you don't. I'm really a horrible person. Save yourself some time and walk away." I retorted, taking my keys out of my pocket to hit the keypad unlocking my door.

"Damn, it's like that?" He grilled, stopping and throwing his hands up as if he was offended.

"It is, but look at it as me saving you. I'm doing you a favor. I'd just ruin your life. You're welcome!" I added as I closed the door, hit my push start and sped off.

"Aaaaawwwww, hell naw!!!" One of his friends blurted out, and the group just bust out laughing.

Mr. Skinny Sag then just swung his hand towards

my car as it sped away yelling "Forget you then!" like I had done something wrong.

Why did men do that? First of all, why are you guys hanging out at a store midday, on a Monday? Don't you have a job? Secondly, if a woman seems uninterested in a conversation, ten times out of ten she isn't interested. She isn't playing hard to get, or the no means yes game, she actually means no, so walk away with your dignity and leave her alone. Lastly, why when men get dissed, they have to act like they didn't want the woman when they just practically stalked her for the last five minutes. Stop trying to prove stuff to your friends. I'm pretty sure your feelings are hurt but as long as she respected you, respect that she just isn't interested. She isn't a nappy headed slut or raggedy bitch just because she rejected you. Grow up and learn how to accept rejection. Everyone gets rejected, deal with it.

I must've been mental ranting quite a bit because by the time I snapped out of it, I was pulling up to my neighborhood gate. I couldn't wait to lay down and watch rachet show Monday and laugh at reality show drama in order to get my mind off my own. There was nothing like a Love and Hip Hop fight even though I knew most of it was scripted.

As I pulled up to my place, I noticed a car that looked familiar from the distance. Once I got closer, I saw a physique that I recognized sitting on the car.

"FUCK MY LIFE!!!" I fumed, as I flipped my head back and closed my eyes tight with frustration.

There Mo was, sitting on his car in front of my house. He looked like he had been waiting there for a while. I didn't know why because I hadn't responded to any of his calls or texts, so I don't know how he knew I was coming home. I parked my car and got out with my purse and bag of wine. I planned to speed walk right by him, and act like he didn't exist. I went to take my first speed step and he walked right in front of me. I then did a quick ball change to get around him.

"Arianna, don't do that. I came to talk to you. I know I owe you an explanation, just talk to me please." He pleaded with me from behind because I had already gotten to my door and put my key in the lock.

He ran up to me just as I was about to close the door, and pushed it open. He then walked in behind me. I proceeded to sit my wine on the counter and my purse alongside it. I grabbed a bottle of wine, and opened it. I then proceeded to drink it out of the bottle and stared at him waiting to hear what he had to say. When he just looked at me with stupid puppy dog eyes, I decided I would begin the conversation.

"Congratulations Maurice, I mean if that's your real name, on your new baby girl. You'll have a beautiful family, I'm sure."

Mo sighed deeply and dropped his head. "Arianna, I promise I didn't mean for any of this to happen. I'm so sorry."

"Oh, I know that. But how did you even know that I knew? When the fuck were you going to tell me you had a whole baby on the way?" I was livid as I yelled at him while still holding my bottle of wine.

"Well, the pictures were posted on my Facebook after I was tagged in them on Saturday. I thought you found out like everyone else, by social media." he admitted, slowly walking towards me.

"Negro don't you take another step! I don't want you near me!" I backed away. "So, you mean to tell me, rather than tell me the full truth, you'd let me find out like everyone else, after being posted on social fucking media." I dropped my head and laughed. "You ain't shit, my nigga! You just like all them other fuck boys! Get the fuck out my house." I demanded, pointing at the door.

"No, Arianna, I know you're mad, but I need you to hear me out. Amber and I weren't together when I met you. We had been broken up for five months. I had no knowledge of the pregnancy because we hadn't spoken since the breakup. I really thought it was over. Then two weeks ago, she calls me crying, said she just found out she was seven months pregnant. She claimed that she wasn't having any symptoms, nor was she showing until then. I didn't want to deal with it at first, but then I realized that if she was seven months pregnant, then it was mines. I couldn't just let her raise the baby alone, so I called her back and now we're figuring it out. I never meant to hurt you, I promise." Mo justified sincerely.

I took my wine and placed it in my arm and began clapping. "Let's give it up for Maurice everybody, baby daddy of the fucking year."

Mo smacked his teeth "You can't be serious right now. You think this shit is funny?!" He spat, cocking his head to the side and squinting trying to figure out why I was clapping.

"No, but I think you're a joke. All that shit is fine and dandy, but you don't keep the person you're dating in the dark about some shit like that. You were supposed to alert me as soon as you decided that you were going to work it out with her. Instead, you let two fucking weeks go by like you and I were just peachy keen. Meanwhile, you were planning an entire fucking family!!!!!!" I launched the bottle of wine across the room, and it shattered all over the wall. I then placed my hands in my face and began crying uncontrollably.

Mo was shocked, and quickly ran over to hold me. I jerked my entire body back "Go! Just go! Be a good dad to your little girl."

"But, Ari—" Mo tried to talk, but I interrupted him again.

"GO!!!!" I yelled, and pointed towards the door.

Mo looked at me one last time, and I saw a tear

drop from his eye. He then turned his back and walked out of the door. My heart broke into a million pieces seeing the man I was deeply in love with close the door. I fell to the floor and I just cried. I cried for Mo, I cried for my broken heart, and I cried for the past pains I had gone through that left me in an even more broken place. I was so weak. I couldn't get myself up from the floor, all I could was cry.

Knock knock knock

"Who the hell could that be?" I thought to myself. I was way too weak to get up from the floor, so I hoped they'd go away. I then heard the doorknob twist, and I instantly looked up in fear. Then I saw someone peek their head in.

"Arianna, are you alright?" Keith inspected nervously. I had no idea why he was there, but a part of me was really happy to see him.

He looked over to see me planted on the floor, then he quickly ran over. "Arianna! Are you alright? Did he hurt you? I'm about to fuck him up!" Keith panicked thinking someone had caused me harm.

I laughed through my tears. "No, no, calm down,

crazy. Nothing is broken on me, but my heart." I confessed with my head still facing the floor. I turned to look at Keith with curiosity. "Wait, how did you know a he was even in here?"

"I came over to apologize one more time since our conversation at the comedy club went left, but when I got out the car I heard commotion coming from your place. I then saw a guy rush out, and get into his Benz and speed off. I didn't know what was going on so I had to come make sure you were good. That's why I just came right in when you didn't come to the door." Keith explained with concern in his eyes. "But let me get you up off the floor." Keith took his strong hands and lifted my entire body off of the floor.

It felt so good to be held, so I just wrapped my arms around his neck and rested my head on his chest. He then proceeded to the couch and tried to place me down. "No, can you just hold me for a minute?" I looked into his eyes hoping he'd have sympathy for me.

He looked at me shocked that I actually wanted him to hold me and shook his head up and down quickly "Yes, of course ba—I mean Arianna. I got you, I always got you." He then kissed me on the forehead and sat down with me in his lap. He looked down at me and smiled, as if he had been waiting on this moment.

I started laughing again and he looked at me confused. "What the hell are you laughing at?" he asked.

"You remember that time we went white water rafting, and they flipped the boat?"

He nodded his head and smiled, "Yea, I remember."

"I went in super panic mode and thought I was drowning in real life, and I was only under the water about one foot. You jumped in to save me, and my scary ass pushed you down to save myself." We both started cracking up.

"Yep. I'm over here trying to save you, and you're trying to drown me."

"Every man for hisself when you drowning bruh."

"You crazy." he shook his head and smiled. "But I was serious when I said I always got you. I had you then, and I got you now." He looked into my eyes adoringly.

In that moment, I felt safe again. I knew it was

because I was so broken up over Mo, but I didn't care. I was happy that Keith was there. This was the best I felt since Saturday. Before he could say another word, I kissed him. We began to kiss passionately, and he wrapped his strong arms around me and pulled me closer. I proceeded to extend one of my legs over his body and straddle him. I grabbed his head and kissed him deeper. He pulled me closer to him and gripped me firmly. He took his hands and slid them down my Georgia peach and squeezed it. I felt my waterfall begin to flow. Then I remembered a very important part of the weekend; I hadn't showered since Saturday. I immediately stopped and jumped off his lap.

"What's wrong? Did I move too fast? I'm sorry, I just thought…" Keith started a nervous ramble.

"No, no." I giggled, "Chill, I just need to run to the restroom really quick. I'll be right back." I winked and scurried off.

As I was walking to the restroom, I heard my phone ring on the bar. I grabbed it as I rushed to the restroom. I recognized the number; it was my doctor's office. Without thinking, I just picked up the phone.

"Hello, Ms. Hill, how are you?" asked the nurse.

"I'm fine, what do I owe the pleasure of this call?" I asked, hoping she'd make it quick because I had Keith waiting.

"Well, I'm calling to discuss the results of your last visit."

"Mmm, hhmm." I said hoping she'd hurry up and get to the point.

"Well, your Pap smear came out normal, but your STD screening read that you have gonorrhea. It's nothing to worry about because it's curable, but I'd like to schedule an appointment for you to get treatment as soon as possible."

I heard my cellphone hit the floor and I suddenly got nauseous. I began to sweat and the room was spinning. I almost passed out, but I gripped the bathroom sink before I went down.

"Did she just say I have gonorrhea?"